Upon a Misty Skye

A Novella

Terri Brisbin

Upon a Misty Skye

Acknowledgments

Thanks to Kathryn LeVeque, Eliza Knight, Madeline Martin and Ruth A. Casie – for including me in the wonderful anthology – ONCE UPON A HAUNTED CASTLE – and for their help and inspiration as we wrote these stories.

Dedication

To Sue-Ellen Welfonder and our friend Lisa Trumbauer who took me to Duntulm Castle on my first trip to Scotland and to Skye all those years ago. It was informative and fun to be there with writers who saw the possibilities. I will always be grateful for those days in Scotland!

PROLOGUE

Duntulm Castle
Trotternish, Isle of Skye

A storm raged that night.

Lightning flashed and thunder crashed, illuminating the isles in the Minch. Rain fell in curtains, flooding the beach and covering the rocks beneath the castle. Neither man nor creatures could withstand the power of this storm, but she could.

Agneis MacDonald moved through the ruins, crying out her torment to the angry sky above her. With each scream came an answer from the storm for she was the one who brought the storm here.

Floating through the stone walls as she never could in her mortal life, Agneis stood there and searched the cliffs below her window … again. Not even the brightness of the lightning helped her.

The bairn was gone.

Gone.

One moment in her arms and the next … gone.

Agneis moved back through the walls and sought the lower chambers of the remains of the keep. She wrapped her arms around herself and moaned out the relentless pain. The thick stone walls held most of it in, but a few sounds echoed into the storm and thunder answered her.

At least the bairn died quickly and his spirit traveled on due to his innocence. That was the only mercy God showed that day to anyone named MacDonald.

Turning and twisting, she raced through Duntulm, through the chambers where she had lived and worked and loved that bairn as though he was her own. But always, Agneis returned to that damned window on nights like this. The storm called to her, mocking her and condemning her as her master had that night.

As her mistress collapsed at the news, her master had cursed her in life and death. To never have peace as he would never. To mourn the loss of the wee boy even as he did. Then he had her set afloat in the storm with no oars in the small boat, sentencing her to the same death as his son.

But hers took seven days.

The storm took her far out to sea where she faced the terrible sun and thirst and hunger. Then, as she lay near death, the winds of vengeance blew up waves that threw the boat into the rocks beneath Duntulm. Agneis died in almost the exact spot where the bairn had met his death.

Now, her soul would spend eternity wracked by guilt and grief. Her punishment for naught but a moment's weakness was to never find release from this place. Or from her culpability in the bairn's death.

Days turned into months and then into years and decades and centuries and still she was not released to find peace. Though others visited the castle even when it became ruined and fell apart, no one could see her. Och aye, they could hear her and see the storms she called.

Agneis understood the truth of it—she had never been shriven before set upon the sea. Without a chance to confess her sin and ask for absolution, her soul was damned to never leave this place. She would pay the price for eternity.

Unless …

CHAPTER 1

Dunvegan Castle, Isle of Skye
In the Year of Our Lord 1500

"Father!" Isabel yelled once more at the locked door. "I pray you let me out!" Frustrated, she screamed out even louder. "Father!"

Isabel MacLeod's hands hurt from pounding on the thick wooden door. No matter how many times she had yelled or slammed against it, it did not give way. Nor would, she suspected, her father. Leaning against the door and catching her breath, Isabel knew how stubborn he could be when his temper was high.

And her declaration that she would not marry his choice in marriage had done exactly that. Not even her mother's soothing voice and supplication had changed her sire's mind on his decision—neither the one about whom he had chosen nor the one about her punishment for not obeying him.

Ranald MacLeod would never relent on this. She had insulted his honor before their clan. As she turned and slid down the surface of the door to sit on the floor, Isabel understood her mistake. Too late, it would seem, to do anything about it. Her throat and her palms throbbed as she considered her actions and her choices. Pushing the hair out of her face, Isabel glanced around the now empty chamber and realized she had little to choose.

Stripped of every comfort, her bedchamber was emptied on her father's orders. Her clothing, trunks, jewelry and belongings were gone. Her bed was gone and two blankets lay thrown in the corner for her use. He had even ordered the shutters removed from the window so that the cold sea winds would have no barriers. The MacLeod wanted his daughter to suffer for her refusal to bow to his wishes. When a strong burst of wet wind filled the chamber, she climbed to her feet to rescue the blankets.

As she stood in the center of her room, Isabel did ken that being held prisoner in this place was her biggest obstacle. No one would help her while she was being punished by her father. She began pacing around the chamber, staying as far from the window as she could. Her thoughts came more easily when she moved and it took little time to come up with a plan.

First, she must get free of this chamber.

Then, she would send word to Alexander.

Finally, she and Alexander would escape their fathers' demands and control.

Isabel was not clear yet on the how and the where of it, but she trusted that Alex would have a plan by the time he helped her escape Dunvegan and her father.

Somehow.

A few hours passed before she called out to the guard her father had left outside her door, asking for her father's forgiveness. No response came that night or the two days following. With only a jug of water left for her use and no food, she was weak and cold when the door opened and her father entered. From the victorious smirk that lay across his stony face and her mother's worried expression as she peeked into the chamber, Isabel knew her punishment was not over yet.

"Bring her to the hall. My daughter can beg my forgiveness in the place where she insulted me."

Two guards entered and took her by the arms and she was dragged down the stairs from her chamber in the west tower. After two and more days exposed to the cold and wind without food, she had not the strength to oppose the guards. And when they stopped at the front of the chamber and her father took his place there in the huge chair reserved for him, their hold was the only thing keeping her on her feet.

Isabel tried to put words together in her thoughts, to prepare herself to apologize, but terror filled her as she watched her father nod to someone behind her. She had seen the expression on his face before and it did not bode well for her. Daring a glance over her shoulder, she watched as the huge giant of a man called Gair strode forward and stopped just a pace behind her.

"My daughter has insulted my honor before all of you," her father called out. Isabel's body trembled. "A recalcitrant daughter is something no man should bear." Without realizing it, Isabel began tugging against the guards' hold on her. "Certainly not the chieftain of the Clan MacLeod."

As many voices called out in his support, her father nodded to Gair who grabbed the back of her gown and tore it open with only his hands.

"Father, I pray you," she called out. "Forgive me!"

Isabel knew what came next. She had witnessed it many times, usually when kith or kin misbehaved and sometimes when they willfully disobeyed.

Willful disobedience.

Her throat tightened and shudders coursed through her then, causing the guards to strengthen their grasp of her arms. With one final tear, her gown fell open exposing her entire back to those watching. Naked now from her shoulders to her feet, she realized the punishment to come.

Whipping. He would have her whipped with a lash.

"My lord?" Gair said, his voice sending shivers through her.

"Ten, Gair," he ordered. "And do not hold back because she is my daughter."

"Aye, my lord," Gair said, dropping the length of his whip and shaking it free. He snapped it in the air next to her a few times and she could not help but tremble each time.

"You there, hold her head up so I can see her face." The guard on her left took hold of her hair and pulled it tightly, forcing her face up.

"Father, I beg your forgiveness. I ken I was wrong. I pray you …"

Gair waited not for any further instructions, striking quickly. The leather strip struck against her back, its tip stinging her skin. She gasped. Then Isabel gritted her teeth and tried to ready herself for the next one. No preparation would have helped for Gair delivered it to the same place, worsening the pain. She closed her eyes and waited for the third. The guard pulled hard on her hair.

"Open your eyes, Daughter," her father called out. "I would see yours as you receive your just punishment." The blow came quickly then, forcing a scream out even as she met her father's gaze. The next one landed in the same spot and tore the skin there.

Tears streamed down her cheeks in spite of her attempts to control herself.

Gair was a master at making punishment go quickly or making it last an ungodly amount of time. So, which would it be for her? Could she survive this? More importantly, could the bairn she suspected she carried within live through it?

She had no more time to think on anything as Gair increased the timing and the power behind each stroke. Isabel dared not look away from her father during the rest and he seemed pleased by her screams of pain. Her back, her hips, her buttocks and her legs throbbed in excruciating pain. Blood now trickled down from the open slashes across her body. Gair finished the ten, breathing heavily behind her as he waited for more orders.

"What have you to say, Daughter?" her father voice echoed across the now silent hall.

Her throat dry from too long without water and her voice hoarse from screaming, Isabel forced out the words. Her life depended on it now.

"I will do your bidding, Father. Forgive me for my insult."

No sounds save those of her panting breaths and Gair's labored ones could be heard as they waited to learn if The MacLeod was satisfied with her plea.

"Seat my daughter in her place at table," her father said quietly. "She can join us at supper."

He knew she could not move on her own. He had withheld food for more than two days and she should be ravenous. But the waves of pain and the smell and feel of the blood that now dripped down her back and legs made her want to retch and fall unconscious.

"My lord husband," her mother's voice broke into her growing confusion now. Where had she been? Why had she not tried to intervene? Isabel knew why. "May I have her washed and dressed as is appropriate for your table?"

'Twas an attempt to see to her, but one even Isabel understood would fail. Ranald MacLeod would make certain that the humiliation and pain lasted longer than this rather brief amount the whipping took.

"Nay, wife. She stays as she is until I say otherwise. Her stubborn nature must be taught a lesson."

The guards dragged her forward, up the steps to her chair on her father's left. She could not help but cry out when they dropped her onto its hard seat. Grasping the edge of the table for support, Isabel tried to find a less painful position but 'twas impossible. When her father approached and stood behind her, she pushed herself to her feet by sheer will alone and waited for him to sit.

He dragged out the meal, giving her a cup of water when wine or a stronger spirit could have aided with the pain. A crust of bread was the only piece of food on her plate, but she could not eat even that. Words blurred together around her. She blinked against the shadowy people as they moved in front of her and spoke to her father. When she could no longer hold herself up, he smiled. As she slumped off the chair towards the floor, Isabel began praying.

"Take her away."

Her prayer continued through the next dark days and nights, even as she cried out in pain as her wounds were treated. She entreated any saint or holy person who would hear her prayers to let her live. Whether it was their intercession or the Almighty's plans or her own stubbornness, she did survive.

Five days after her father's punishment, Isabel could stand on her own and tolerate garments on her skin. She knew she must find a way to contact Alex. Since her own serving maid had been replaced with a woman who shared her father's bed, Isabel had to be even more careful in her actions and words.

Seven days after her humiliation in the hall, her mother brought word that she was to be married to The MacKinnon's heir in three weeks' time.

And seven days later, she realized that her monthly courses had been missing for two months and that child she carried still lived within her.

The MacLeod would not take that news well if he discovered his daughter had lost her virtue under his own watch.

CHAPTER 2

Castle Knock, Isle of Skye
One Week Later

Alexander MacDonald, second son to the chieftain, strode into the hall just as his father burst into loud and raucous laughter. Alex had been waiting for his return for weeks and now he had arrived. His matter could wait no longer, but as he watched, his father leaned over and slapped Alex's older brother on the back.

"Can you imagine it, Connor?" Eoin MacDonald asked, glee filling his voice. "Can you see it?" The others there, elders and the chieftain's men, laughed.

"I cannot, but I wish I had," Connor answered. Alex reached the front of the large chamber and nodded to those gathered.

"Oh, Alex, you canna believe the news we just heard," his father's face grew red as he laughed once more. "Go on with you, Brodie. Tell Alex what you heard."

Brodie was a cousin and one usually set to watch over the MacLeod's comings and goings. From the look of him now, he had ridden and sailed hard and long to reach Sleat from the far west of Skye. Distrust had long reigned between the two powerful clans who each claimed control of huge sections of the isle and the mainland of Scotland as well. Now though, fear filled Alex's heart and a strange tightness in his stomach began as the man spoke for his own matter involved that clan on the other side of Skye.

"The MacLeod's daughter defied him in his own hall!" Brodie said. Everyone there laughed again, including his father, but Alex felt no glee at this news. Not when …

"Defied him in what matter?" Alex asked. He hoped his interest was not showing in his tone of voice.

"Does it matter, lad?" one of the elders asked. "No one naysays The MacLeod and lives."

"He ordered her to marry a man of his choosing and she refused! Stood right in front of him and the rest of them and refused." Brodie crossed his arms over his massive chest in a mocking action, showing how the girl had done it. "But, Robbie," he nodded at the elder who'd spoken as Alex's gut twisted, "the lass yet lives." Brodie shrugged. "Well, she did when

I left there two days ago. Whipped bloody for her refusal, but bowing and scraping now."

Dear God in Heaven, what had happened? When he had left her, he'd promised to come back and claim her. He just needed to make his case to his own father and gain his support so they could be together. His father had not been at Knock though. Alex discovered that he had been on his own journey and only arrived back this morn. And now, this?

"She's worth more as a marriage boon than a dead one," someone else called out.

"A ruthless bastard he may be," his father said. "But he kens her value. He made his point and she learned it, fear not."

A few nods and words from all of those present over The MacLeod's ruthlessness, his iron rule and his understanding of the value of his daughter followed as Alex struggled to keep his tongue behind his teeth.

He needed a plan and he needed it now. As usual, no one noticed as he left his father and the rest while Brodie was finishing his report of the recent activities at Dunvegan and on the MacLeod lands.

Or so he thought.

"What did you do?" Connor asked, coming up behind him and grabbing his shoulder to slow him down. Alex crossed his arms over his chest and shrugged.

"I did nothing." Connor shook his head as one side of his mouth lifted in a smirk.

"Nothing is it? Someone who does not ken you might believe it, but I ken you, Brother. I've been with you when you get on the wrong side of trouble." Connor's gaze narrowed. His brother was tenacious when something teased his curiosity. "Then why did you go as pale as Granny's skin when Brodie talked about the lass?"

Alex considered his options. His brother could not keep anything secret. Connor had never been able to stay silent in his whole life and Alex had been punished many, many times because of his older brother's loose tongue. Still, he could use an ally in whatever he needed to do to get to Isabel and his brother might be one.

"I ken the MacLeod lass."

Other than a narrowing of his gaze, Alex could not tell Connor's reaction to his words. His older sibling was not stupid, so Alex knew he would understand it soon. A swift indrawn breath told Alex the moment Connor had.

"Ken?" Connor's gaze grew both knowing and intense. "In the biblical sense or in the 'you passed her in the village and greeted her' way?" When Alex did not reply right away, Connor shook his head and laughed. "Good Christ! You have a way of walking into piles of shite, do you not, Brother?"

"I must … I have to …" he began without truly knowing how much to reveal. His brother held up his hand and shook his head.

"First, tell me nothing," Connor advised. "Then, if Father asks me about your absence or your actions or your plans, I will be able to truthfully answer that I knew not of them. Unless you want him to ken?"

When had his brother realized his failing? Alex could not remember Connor's acknowledgement of his weakness in the past, but he was glad of it at this moment.

"If you had not left the hall when you did, you would have heard Father order Brodie back to Dunvegan to discover who The MacLeod betroths her to. There has been speculation for some time over which clan he will ally himself with using her hand in marriage."

"Who does Father think it will be?" Alex asked. He needed to ken who his enemies would be when he claimed Isabel.

"There was a half-hearted attempt to put me forward some months ago. Talk of a formal peace between us and such," Connor explained. Brother or no, he could feel the anger build at the thought of such a match. Connor waved him off. "Could be the MacKinnons or even the Macleans of Mull."

He was already so late in returning to her. He had promised her that he would speak to his father, gain his support and then bring her home. Never expecting The MacLeod to move so swiftly towards a betrothal with someone else, he had waited for his father to return. And knowing Isabel as he did, he understood that she would not quietly acquiesce to her father's demands, not even to gain time for Alex to act.

Sometimes he wished she could be a meek lass. He smiled then, remembering all the reasons he was pleased she was not so. If she had been, they would never have met and never would have loved. They would never have…

"Alex!" His name shouted from down the corridor caught his attention and he turned as Brodie rushed towards him and Connor. "I must speak wi' ye."

"And I must leave," Connor said. With a nod, his brother turned and left quickly, passing Brodie without another word.

Alex motioned to Brodie to follow him outside. Once in the yard, he led the man to a place away from the keep and closer to the stables. Assured that no one was close enough to overhear their words, Alex nodded.

"A lass approached me outside Dunvegan."

"Was it The MacLeod's daughter?" he asked. Was she even well enough after such a punishment?

"Nay. That one goes nowhere without several servants and a guard behind her now."

"Now?"

"Aye, now. Once she rose from her bed and begged her father's pardon again-,"

"Again?" Alex grabbed Brodie's cloak and pulled him closer. "What do you mean 'again'?"

"Well, he locked the lass away for several days when she refused him. When she agreed to beg his pardon, he had her whipped and then let her agree to obey him."

The bile rose in his gut and he sickened at the thought that he had left Isabel to the questionable mercies of her father. Why had she not simply given in? She must ken he would find a way to her side. She must.

"You said a lass approached you?" Alex brought the talk back to its subject.

"Aye." Brodie reached inside his tunic and pulled out a small square of fabric. "She asked me to bring this to ye. And not to tell anyone else about it." Alex held out his hand and Brodie placed it there.

"And did you? Tell anyone?"

"Nay," he said with a broad smile. "She made it worth my while to do her bidding." Then he shrugged. "Besides, I care not who ye tup, MacLeod or other."

Alex turned away and opened the small package, finding a folded piece of parchment within the layers of cloth. Her words were curt and dire. He would have only days to get there and get her out of Dunvegan and away from her father. He was to seek out the kitchen maid who had given this note to Brodie when he arrived. No words of love, though truly none could be risked in such a communication.

"When do you return there?" Alex asked as he turned to face the man.

"On the morrow." Brodie stared at him for a moment before shaking his head. "Does this have anything to do with her? With The MacLeod's daughter?"

"I am coming with you," Alex said, ignoring the other's question. "I will meet you at dawn."

"Alex! God Almighty, tell me ye are not tupping the MacLeod's daughter!" Brodie blocked his path and grabbed him by his shoulders. "Ye would not be that stupid, would ye?"

"At dawn," he said, pulling free from the man's hold. "And bring a few trusted men, I will need help."

Brodie relented in his questions when he realized Alex would say no more on the matter of The MacLeod's daughter. But the truth of this was much worse than that.

Alex had married The MacLeod's only daughter and heir.

The next morning found him and a small group of men aboard the small birlinn that would take him north and west to the edge of Skye and to Dunvegan. Brodie would take his place back in the village outside the keep and watch for the kitchen maid who had so pleasurably given him orders to bring the message to Alex. Alex had come up with a plan, a dangerous one, and he prayed that he would arrive in time to save his wife from whatever else her father could do to her.

CHAPTER 3

"She is in the tower there, nearest the cliff," Brodie explained. "The maid said she is accompanied at all times by the laird's leman and has a guard posted at her door."

"So her father trusts her not?"

"Just so."

Brodie nodded and turned away, blocking Alex as several MacLeod warriors passed them. For safety's sake, Alex lowered his head and tugged his hood down over his forehead. He could take no risk of being recognized here and now.

"The leman sleeps in her chamber or returns to The MacLeod's bed?"

"Lara says she remains in the lady's chamber. I would guess the chieftain is not happy over the lack of a warm body in his sheets."

"Lara is it then?" Alex watched the ruddy man's face color even more at his question. For all his burliness and rough ways, Brodie had a soft heart for the lasses. Much as Alex had until he had met Isabel that day some months ago.

"Aye. Lara."

Alex left that alone for now. He knew that Isabel's father would guard his daughter against any possible further disobedience. The presence of the woman in her chamber was a difficulty but one he must overcome. The moon would be dark on the morrow's night, so that was their best chance of escape without being seen.

"We make our way past the guards by bringing in a wagon of goods for the kitchen and then hide until nightfall," he repeated to Brodie. "Lara will get the sleeping draught to Isabel. Once the leman and the guard sleep, we will get to her chamber and get her the hell out."

It sounded so simple and yet it was a plan riddled with the possibility of failure. And failure meant death for him and, most likely, for his wife and any who dared defy The MacLeod. Brodie studied Alex for several silent moments before shrugging and nodding. That was the blunt man's way of agreeing. Now, they need only wait until the morrow and then find the wagon and ride it into the keep.

Alex and Brodie walked down the pathway away from the gates and guards and turned a corner heading towards the place where the maid's brother would wait for them at midday on the morrow. Although Brodie seemed willing to trust the maid and her willingness to be part of this, Alex knew that the small sack of coins inside his tunic would ease their way for both the brother's help and any else who needed gold to convince them.

As they walked, something made Alex look at the keep. There, in the small window on the tower closest to the cliff, he saw Isabel, her blond hair streaming around her from the breezes. So small due to the distance, Alex could not be certain she gazed at him, but he pushed back his hood and nodded to her, hoping she saw him. He watched as she pushed open the window and leaned her face out of it.

I am coming, Isabel. Wait for me.

He sent the thought up to her, praying her heart would hear it and ken he had not forsaken her. When she turned away and tugged the window closed, he knew not if she had.

Damn, but waiting for another day before he could take her from here to safety would nearly kill him.

It was Alex!

Isabel fought not to reveal her joy and relief as she closed the window as Evanna ordered her to do. Her message had made it to him and Alex was here to help her. She took a deep breath, pushed her hair over her shoulders and turned to face the dreadful woman in her chamber.

"I did not realize how cold it was when I opened the window," she said softly. "Pardon." She longed to grind her teeth over the insult of this woman's presence near her, but the whipping had taught her to resist her impatient urges.

What her father saw in this woman of plain features and a nasty disposition, Isabel knew not. Even with her auburn hair arranged neatly and a new gown covering her curves, Isabel saw nothing that should appeal to a man like her father. He usually favored women with dark hair and voluptuous curves. And women who raised not their voices to question or to plead or to request. This one, though, was none of those things.

Isabel used all her control to nod in a polite way at her father's whore and walk to the chair in the corner. Picking up her embroidery, she let her thoughts free even as her fingers flew over the fabric, weaving a plan as her threads wove a pattern. She must wait on his word, though how it would reach her, she knew not.

The silence grated on Evanna's nerves, Isabel realized, and the woman grew more moody with every hour she spent here, banished from Isabel's father's bed and forced to watch over his daughter.

Whatever threat or promise her father had made to his leman must have been serious and impressive for her to accept this absence.

Even though it was not a topic worthy or appropriate for the chieftain's unwed daughter, Evanna made no secret of her appetite for pleasures of the flesh. There was not a woman in the keep or village of Dunvegan who had not heard the stories of excess. Most likely, even The MacLeod's wife was privy to the knowledge of it, for neither the chief nor his lover practiced discretion around Elizabeth Matheson, Lady MacLeod.

Another hour passed before she calmed enough to slow her work. A glance around the chamber revealed that her gaoler had fallen asleep in her chair. Isabel rested her hands and the fabric and needle on her lap and let out her breath for the first time all day.

He was here.

Though a good distance sat between them, she would have—and did—recognize him even so. Isabel would admit, only to herself, that a small bit of doubt had entered her heart during the worst moments in these last weeks. He had promised his love, his name and his protection, but here, deep in The MacLeod's control and demesne, she did worry. Murmured promises in the dark were not always the most reliable; she had both understood and feared that.

Now, a peace filled her for no matter what

happened, they would face it together. Her hand slipped down over her belly before she could stop and only the knock at the door startling her saved the gesture from being seen by Evanna. The woman woke with a start and glared at Isabel as though she was the cause of the disruption. Finally remembering that she was not the nobleborn woman in the chamber, Evanna walked to the door and lifted the latch.

"You are late," she scolded as she pulled it open wide. The guard standing there turned to watch the kitchen maid enter. From the way he sniffed at the tray the girl carried, he must be hungry as well. "Put it there." With a pointing finger, Evanna directed the servant to the table before the hearth.

As the girl passed Isabel, she stumbled and the tray tilted. Several bowls and cups slid over its edge as the servant tried to right it. Isabel jumped to her feet to help while Evanna simply yelled out in anger.

"Are you daft?" she called out without ever trying to help.

"Evanna, that will do no good," Isabel began as she grabbed on to the edges of the large, wooden tray to steady it. "Let me help you."

The girl stuttered something as she gained her balance. As Isabel knelt to gather the spilled bowls and cups, she felt Lara slide something into her hand. The glance the girl gave told her to be silent about it. Isabel stood and stepped back, closing her fingers over the mysterious bit.

"Go! Get fresh food or send someone back who is not a clumsy fool if you cannot carry it yourself," Evanna ordered.

For one so dependent on the whims of a man and who could face banishment or humiliation at any time, Evanna seemed to forget her true place and to revel in her momentary power. Isabel hid the smile that crept onto her own lips, knowing that this one would face a downfall.

Lara placed the bowls and cups on the table there and then made her way out of the chamber quickly, with a few more mumbled apologies and a wink at Isabel when Evanna had turned away. Isabel slipped the tiny packet inside her sleeve and thought on how best to open it in privacy. The place where Evanna hated the most and tended to drift away from constant observation was the chapel. Determined to seek it out, Isabel walked to the table and took a cup of ale and piece of bread.

"She had better bring more stew," Evanna whispered with a nod at the closed door.

"I am not that hungry right now," she said, holding up the bread. "This is enough for me."

It took almost more patience than she thought existed within her to wait for more food to arrive and for her miserable overseer to finish it. Isabel bided quietly until she thought she had reached the perfect moment and then stood. Evanna frowned, watching her.

"Before I seek my rest, I wish to go to the chapel."

She said it firmly and waited. Both she and Evanna had been present when her father had made it clear that being in the chapel, on her knees and begging God's forgiveness for her headstrong ways was one of few acceptable behaviors he condoned right now.

"Can you not wait until the morn?" Evanna asked, crossing her arms over her meager chest.

"You need not attend me," Isabel offered as she lifted the latch and pulled. "The guard will nip at my heels in your stead, if you prefer to wait for me here."

The guard turned at her words and bowed, waiting on her word. Humiliated and whipped before all to see, she had expected more scorn and shame from those here. But this guard, as well as any others who attended or spoke to her, showed only respect.

"My lady?" he asked.

"I am going to the chapel to pray," she explained, with a glance back over her shoulder at the displeased woman there.

"Have ye a cloak? The rains started earlier," he offered.

With a nod, she lifted her hooded cloak from a peg on the wall and stepped out of the chamber. She may have to endure the leman's constant company, but Isabel had not been made a prisoner. Just uncomfortable. Pausing for a moment, she waited for Evanna to speak or follow her. With a muttered curse, the woman came along.

Isabel must discover Alex's plan. She must be ready for whatever happened. It took less time than she thought for Evanna to lose interest and wander outside of the damp, chill, stone room. With only one door to enter and leave, her guard remained just outside. The priest had already retired for the night, his snores echoed out from the small chamber behind the altar telling her she would not be disturbed by him.

It took little time to read his message and his plan and to understand her part in it. It took much longer and more effort to tamp down her anticipation and to appear well-prayed and ashamed when she left the chapel and returned to her chamber.

The night and next day took months to pass, or so it seemed. Finally, the sun slid below the horizon and no moon rose and Isabel did as Alex bade her do. When both the leman and the guard lay soundly and deeply asleep, she waited for his arrival.

CHAPTER 4

Alex crept out of the storage chamber off the kitchen, making sure he avoided any of the servants who yet toiled there. Brodie followed behind him, his sure steps and presence giving Alex more confidence in this plan than he felt right now. Even knowing the others waited outside the gates to help their escape did not help.

Making their way from here up to Isabel's tower room was not a sure thing and filled with any number of dangers and challenges. He cleared his thoughts of all but one—his wife needed him.

As Lara described, most of those living here in the keep were at their rest and few awake. Due to the arrogance of The MacLeod, few guards stood watch here within his hall or anywhere but the doors leading in or out. Alex and Brodie silently strode along the dark-shadowed walls and up steps until they reached her chamber.

No guard stood there waiting for them.

'Twas either a very good or very bad thing. Only opening the door would reveal the truth. Alex offered up a quick prayer in case the Almighty was listening and lifted the latch. Easing the door open, he heard Brodie behind him, waiting and prepared for whatever lay behind it. Dagger in hand, Isabel stood just inside, her eyes blazing and her body ready to fight, like an avenging angel.

His avenging angel.

"Isabel," he whispered as he and Brodie entered and closed the door behind them. "Isabel."

She dropped the dagger and ran into his open arms. Alex held her, just held her, feeling the breaths entering and leaving her body and letting her heat warm him. He slid his hands up, tangling his fingers into the mass of long, blond curls to draw her head back, and stared at her face.

"Are you well, lass?" he asked. He searched her features and noticed the dark circles beneath her green eyes and the paleness of her skin. "I heard what your father did to you."

"Now that you have returned, it matters not," she whispered before lifting her mouth to his.

Alex accepted and took possession of her lips, slanting just so that she opened to his tongue. He tasted her and suckled her tongue when she offered it to him. She had been crying for the saltiness of tears lay on her lips. But mostly, she tasted like… home.

"Alex," Brodie growled. "We have no time for this."

Alex pulled away from Isabel and nodded. Glancing behind her, next to the bed on the floor, he saw a woman and a man, trussed up like suckling pigs ready for the roast. They did not move at all and barely breathed. Alex smiled at his wife.

"You did well," he said. "How long have they been asleep?" The potion Lara had passed to Isabel would make them sleep like the dead for hours and hours, she had promised.

"Nigh on two hours," she said. "I am afraid my tying skills may not keep them thus." Isabel nodded at the guard. "He is so heavy that I feared I would never move him there."

Brodie walked by Alex and crouched next to the two, tugging at the bonds and gags Isabel had placed. He stood and shrugged.

"They'll do just fine, lady." Brodie nodded at the door. "We should go. Now."

Alex grabbed the leather satchel at her feet and tossed it to Brodie. As he picked up the cloak there on the bed, he noticed that she wore the same gown she had worn when they spoke their vows. Plain, it would garner no attention from anyone seeing it. After he wrapped the cloak around her shoulders, he gathered her in close. Though she tried to hide the pain, he saw it in the tightness around her eyes and mouth.

"I should have been here," he whispered, easing his hold and pressing his lips against her forehead. "I should have stopped it."

She slid her hand into his and squeezed it. "You are here now." Brodie lifted the latch and checked the corridor outside.

"Come."

Alex supported Isabel during the fast-paced run from her chamber, down the stairs and through the long corridors back to the kitchen. She struggled to keep up with their long-legged strides, but never complained or slowed. They reached the kitchen and the storage chamber where he and Brodie had hidden and crept back inside it.

"Why are we stopping here?" Isabel asked, taking in deep breaths as she spoke.

"We will go out as we came in," Brodie explained. "At first light when the gates open."

"I can show you another way out."

Alex glanced at Brodie. They'd planned to hide her in the same wagon they'd used to get into the castle yard and leave as soon as the gates opened in the morn, rousing little suspicion or concern. But every moment they remained here raised the possibility of being discovered. Or that the potion would wear off sooner than expected.

Alex smiled and nodded at his wife. He trusted her

to ken a better way. "Show us."

She could not stop touching him. Now that he was here, Isabel held on to his hand or his arm. In her confusion and pain after the whipping, she had thought of him and him alone. It would be a long time before she would convince herself to loosen her hold on him. Or to stop staring into the blue depths of his eyes. Or to lose the need to kiss him.

"This way," she said, nodding to Brodie to open the door.

It hurt to move quickly. It hurt to wear the heavy, dark cloak that would hide her features and protect her from the cold outside. But, none of that could slow her down or they would both, they would all perish. She stopped and faced the large, rough man who accompanied Alex. He was not what she had expected after Lara's words of praise, but he had carried the message and brought Alex here.

"Brodie?" He nodded and watched her expectantly. "Lara cannot remain behind. My father will kill her for helping me, us, when he discovers this."

"Aye, ye are right on that, lady. Lara waits now at our meeting place. I wi' see her safe."

Alex chose his friends well. She nodded and led them to another storage chamber. There, hidden in the stone wall, was a secret doorway. She counted the stones as her mother had told her to do and pushed on a round one at the top corner of the wall. A soft grating sound was the only noise as the passageway was revealed to them.

Her mother could not openly help Isabel, but in revealing this to her one night as she sat at Isabel's bedside, nursing her bloodied back, her mother had given her a way out of whatever her father planned. Shocked by even that attempt on her mother's part to circumvent her father, Isabel was glad of it now. Once Brodie lit the torch held on the wall inside, she allowed Alex to go ahead, using him for support on the dark steps that led down beneath the keep.

Isabel thought on her mother's words as she walked down through the dark place. This had been carved out of the bedrock of the headlands on which Dunvegan sat at the same time that the oubliette had been dug—that structure hiding this one. Only the chieftain and his most trusted aides knew of this.

And apparently his wife.

They reached the end of this chamber and found another doorway. When Alex pulled it open, they were met by the salty smell of the sea. A sea cave would lead them to the cliff side of the keep and escape. But, according to her mother's words, this path was arduous and long and Isabel could feel her strength waning and each step she took brought collapse closer.

"Rest here, love," Alex said to her, drawing her to

his side and letting Brodie pass. "Go ahead and see what lies there." Isabel slumped against him and gasped when her back hit the stone wall.

"Is there anything I can do?" he asked. Concern laced his words and his gaze.

"Nay. The worst is past, but the skin is tight and yet pulls when I move."

"I will kill him."

She startled at his vehemence. "I do not think either of us can do that, no matter how much we might want it."

"Well, he will never touch you again, Isabel," he swore. "I will make certain that you are safe."

That brought them to the heart of the issue—what would they do once they were away from Dunvegan?

"Where will we go, Alex?" she asked. "What will we do, if we escape?" She brushed her hair back from her face and searched his.

"When we escape." He reached up and touched her cheek, smoothing her hair again. "We will escape. And we will be together. I vowed before God to be at your side, Isabel."

"What did your father say when he heard that we were wed?"

She knew the answer before he said a word, for the guilty look in his dark blue eyes shone there. Their marriage was yet a secret from his family as well as hers. Isabel closed her eyes and then tried to release her frustration and fear as a breath.

"My father will take us in if for no other reason than to thwart and anger yours," he assured.

The thought of facing The MacDonald's ire and his wrath did nothing to ease her mind or heart. She had thought that Alex's return here to rescue her meant he had explained their marriage to his father and his family would accept it and her. Feuding families often married to settle issues and this could be simply one of those. She had hoped. She had prayed. The gentle touch of his hand, lifting her chin so that their gazes could meet, made her open her eyes.

"You are in pain and exhausted. When we get out of here and you are rested and recovered, we will sort it all out."

Isabel was in pain and nights of sleepless tossing and turning had sapped whatever strength she might have had before her father's punishment. The constant fear that her father would discover her secret made her fret through every hour of each day.

For, in spite of her fear that she had lost the bairn inside, she now suspected she had not. Unable to speak openly or ask questions about such things, she could only rely on memories of bits and pieces she had overheard discussed by other women about it. Now, with Alex here, it felt wonderful to have someone else who could take on her burdens and help ease her fears.

Isabel slid her arms under his and rested her head against his strong chest. Her whole body relaxed and even the pressure on her back did not bother her when he embraced her.

They were together. She breathed in his scent, slowly savoring him.

They were together. Isabel stroked her hands up and down the muscles of his back, accepting the strength he offered in his arms.

They were together.

She only knew she had slept when his whispered words woke her. It was time to leave Dunvegan behind and begin their life together.

CHAPTER 5

Alex helped Isabel along the wet path. They needed to reach the top of this embankment of rock before the sun rose or they would be seen. Exposure now meant death. Brodie led the way, testing each step and gaining a new foothold before moving forward. No one spoke aloud and, other than a few whispered words of encouragement, they climbed in silence.

Even though they'd left hours ahead of when they'd planned, it was taking longer than he expected it would to cross the rocks from the mouth of the cave to higher dry land. Still, they would arrive from the other direction and be able to approach the meeting place without coming through the village or from the keep. A good thing to be sure.

Finally, they reached the top and he supported Isabel while she caught her breath. She had not complained once, not even when his hold slipped and his hands pressed into her back. When they could stop, he would see the extent of the damage her father's callousness had wrought. But for now, he simply held her and helped her take each step.

Her expression when she had asked about his family's reaction to news of their marriage still haunted him. Alex would explain it all to her. And beg her forgiveness for not being at her side sooner.

"Alex."

He stopped and waited for Brodie. The man had walked ahead of them to see if there was trouble. He appeared like a ghost out of the swirling mist that formed over the sea and rolled up onto the shore and out through the glens towards the mountains of Skye. Alex shivered at the sight, as though someone had walked across his grave.

"No trouble," Brodie said in a quiet voice. The fog intensified sounds rather than muffling them, so they took care not to make too much noise. "The men are ready."

"What will we do?" Isabel asked him.

"Your father will search for you first in the keep and then the village. If he does not find you, he will then expand outward to the nearby villages and towns. If someone, anyone, connects you to me and the MacDonalds, he will look to the sea and to the south towards our lands when he discovers you missing." Alex pointed into the distance towards his home in Sleat.

"So where can we go?" He smiled at her question and nodded at Brodie.

"We go deeper into MacLeod lands."

"Alex, no," Isabel began to argue with him. "There is no place we can hide from him if we remain here."

"Nay, not here, love. East and then north and west to the other part of Skye that used to be my clan's. There is a place where Brodie can meet us once your father follows the trail my men leave behind."

With the exception of this area and Sleat where his family lived, most of this isle had been fought over and changed hands for centuries. What had belonged to the MacDonalds was now controlled by the MacLeods and the opposite as well. Whether by fighting for it or being granted it by kings and conquerors mattered not and Alex had no doubt that it would continue to happen over the next generations of both clans. Castles, ports, lands and wealth moving back and forth as loyalties, feuds, battles, kingdoms and treaties continued to shift over and over. 'Twas simply the way of things here.

He led her over to the small group gathered by the path to the village. Brodie and three others waited with horses. A young woman who must be Lara stood there, very close to Brodie's side, Alex noticed. The bag Isabel had packed was tied to one of the horses.

"Lara," Isabel said as they approached. "My thanks for your part in this." She reached out and hugged the maid.

"And mine as well, lass," Alex offered.

"Yer lady mother was the one who sent me to find this one, Lady Isabel."

Isabel startled at this news. With no knowledge of who had instigated the first contact, Alex would still never have guessed that Lady MacLeod would have helped.

"My mother?" Isabel glanced from Alex to Brodie and back again. "How? Why?"

"She heard ye whispering things in yer prayers those nights when she sat at yer bedside. Sent me to look for him," she nodded at Brodie.

Of all the things the servant could have said, that news of her mother's part in this shocked her. Never had she intervened on her daughter's behalf before. If Isabel thought her mother's revelation about the secret passage had been a significant thing, then this news was something even more impressive.

But then Isabel realized the scary possibility that she had not kept her own secret during those terrifying and tormented days and nights after the whipping. What else had she spoken during her fevered hours?

"How did she ken to send ye to me?" Brodie asked Lara. Isabel could tell his suspicions were raised now. He nodded to his men to mount up, clearly expecting betrayal or discovery.

"The lady said to look for a ruffian with red hair

who stood waiting near the bay where the boats come in. She said ye would be wearing black," Lara said. Her nervous gaze moved around those gathered there. "She told me yer name. Then when Lady Isabel asked for my help, I knew who ye were."

"How in bloody hell would she ken so much?" Brodie whispered through clenched jaws.

"I told Isabel about you, Brodie." Alex nodded at his friend, his very angry friend. "I told her if she had need of me to get word to you."

"So, the damned MacLeods ken me and ken what I do here then?" Isabel stared as the huge man clenched his fists and tightened his body, preparing for a fight.

"Nay, Brodie," Lara said, stepping right up in front of the warrior even as Isabel wanted to warn her away. "The lady and her mother and me. We are the only ones who ken ye." She placed a small hand on his very large arm. "Ye can trust me."

Silence reigned for a long few moments while this settled on all of them. Isabel reeled at the idea that her mother had helped her in such ways, especially knowing what her father would do if he discovered her actions. Telling her of the passageway under the keep was a bad thing, but actually aiding her in sending a message to Alex was quite another. Her father would see each of these actions as nothing less than a complete betrayal of him.

"I think we need to be on our way," she said quietly. There would be time to think on all the surprising bits once they got to safety. "The morning guard will arrive at my chamber door soon and we must be away from here before that happens."

They said their farewells and Alex helped her up on one of the horses there. It hurt. Every part of her hurt. But, she could not let it slow them down now. She had survived and would do everything she could to remain that way.

Brodie ordered two men to stay in Dunvegan village to keep watch and then climbed up on his massive horse. With a nod at Alex and then at Isabel, he reached down and pulled Lara up behind him on the horse. From her tremulous expression, Isabel doubted the girl had ever ridden at all, but she clutched the huge warrior in her arms and nodded at Isabel with a smile.

Then it was time for her and Alex to leave. She peered up through the swirling mist at Dunvegan Castle behind them. Would she ever return here? Sadness pierced her heart at the thought of leaving home forever. In spite of her father's harshness, she had family here and friends whom she would most likely not see again.

"Isabel?" Alex reached over and touched her leg. "'Twill all work out, I promise you."

"Do you worry that you will never see your kin

again, Alex? If neither family will accept our marriage, will we be outcasts from everyone we ken and love?" Sorrow filled her then and made it difficult to keep the tears from flowing.

"Ah, but my love," Alex whispered, bringing his horse closer and leaning towards her. "I am with the one I love and, together, we will start a new family."

His love for her shone from his eyes as he said the promising words and she began to share her secret with him. But something made her stop. Isabel could not understand why she hesitated and yet she did. Mayhap she did not want to burden him with it until she was certain? Having thought she had lost the babe, she now worried that she would even carry to term. Isabel decided to leave it to another time, a better and safer time for such news to be shared.

Without another word, Alex turned and nodded towards the road. In minutes, she could see nothing behind them as they escaped into the thick fog that hugged the ground. She felt lost for the first time in her life.

Alex saw the distress in her eyes and the paleness of her face. Pain sat there as well and he suspected it was more than the physical discomfort from her father's punishments. She had just learned her mother had helped her and then lost her in the next minute.

The best thing he could do was take her to safety and give her time to adjust to all of this. Though married for several months, if he counted all the hours they had had together, the truth was that they had spent fewer than four days together. So, they needed to learn each other's ways and find a way to be husband and wife openly.

Would his father accept their marriage just to spite hers? 'Twas a possibility, aye, but his father tended to be more pragmatic and would accept or reject it based on what benefit it brought to their clan. His sons were just as much a means to an end as Isabel was to her father.

Alex glanced over at her and marveled in the strength of spirit she had. Living with such a man as her father should have made her fearful of placing herself under another's control. Yet she had accepted his offer of marriage without hesitation. Even after he had revealed his identity. When the instant attraction between two strangers had exploded into something more, Isabel had been his equal. In desire, in passion, in love and in courage.

Now it was his duty to protect her against anyone wishing her harm. Whether that was her father or his or any others set against them mattered not. They had not gone about this in the customary manner, but stealing a bride was a long-standing tradition and he would find a way to make his family accept her.

They rode in silence for several hours, neither rushing nor dawdling so that they attracted no attention from others they met along the road. Their first destination was a small village some miles inland and away from Dunvegan. They would stay for a night or two in the same cottage where they had spent their wedding night. It seemed a fitting place to begin their life together.

Secluded. Private.

He swallowed against his body's response to wanting and needing her then and led her to the cottage by a burn. Alex helped Isabel down from the horse and pulled the bags filled with supplies free. He carried everything inside and then bade her to sit while he saw to the horses. If he rushed a bit or was nervous, he knew it was his need to be with her.

She stood in front of the door, ignoring both the stool there and the pallet in the corner. She eased her cloak off as he entered. He read exhaustion and pain in her every movement, so he rushed to her side and helped her.

"Let me help you," he whispered as he lifted the heavy cloak away from her shoulders. Unable to stop himself, he eased his fingers into her hair and loosened the long braid that kept it under control. Then, he slid his hand up to her head and gently caressed her there.

"That feels wonderful," she said on a breathy exhalation, as she leaned against his fingers. "'Tis about the only place on me that does not hurt right now." He hissed and stopped then, her words a reminder about the punishment she had endured. "Nay! I pray you, do not stop."

She reached up and covered his hand to keep it there. If it gave her pleasure or relief, he would not withhold it even though a grimmer task awaited him. After a few minutes, her head bowed and let his hand drift down her neck towards her shoulders. He was ever watchful for a sign of pain. When she tensed her body the slightest bit, he paused.

"I want to see to your injuries, Isabel."

He waited but she gave no response or reaction. Other than the breaths moving in and out of her body, she made no sound or movement. Then, she lifted her head and glanced at him.

"If you must."

He could have said nay. He could have let it pass. But, truly, Alex could not. He'd worried over what had happened and until he saw it with his eyes and made certain she was healing, he could not be at peace with it.

"Is there a salve or ointment to place on the wounds?" he asked, trying to stem the rising anger and fear in his blood.

He had seen men whipped before, their skin torn and blood pouring down to mix with the dirt. He had seen some maimed for life by such punishment and the worst images had taken hold in his thoughts. Now, he would either confirm the worst or learn better.

She walked to where he had dropped her satchel and reached inside, retrieving a small covered jar. Then she held it out to him.

"My mother had it prepared. It has helped."

Isabel turned her back and he watched as she loosened the laces on her gown and let it slide down over her hips to the floor. She stepped out of it and loosened the shift that hid little in the light of day, even in the dimness of the cottage. Clutching her garments in front of her, she stood for his gaze.

Alex found himself holding his breath as the thin layer of linen dropped away, revealing her form and her flesh to his gaze. He fought for control as the slashing lines and wounds came into view. Alex looked in silence at the terrible results, the damage suffered because of their vow.

Was it worth this? Was he?

He had been the reckless womanizer son, never taking responsibility for his actions, always seeking pleasure. His father had lamented his wayward behavior and lauded his older brother for years. If only Alex could be more like Connor … If only he cared more about his duties … If only…

Now, his actions brought this remarkable woman into his life and put hers in danger. So much suffering because of him. Drawing in a breath, he knew he would be the man she needed. The man he should be.

One who was worthy of such pain and love.

"I ken it is horrible to behold," she whispered in a forlorn voice. "You do not need to do this. Just help me get my shift back up …" She began to reach down.

"Nay," he said. "I am not horrified by you or the sight of you in this condition." He reached out and put his hands on her shoulders. "If I am horrified by anything, it is my failure to return to you. That you had to suffer this, for me and our love." He kissed the back of her neck and she shivered.

"I will get you to safety, Isabel. I will make this right between us." He released her and opened the jar of foul-smelling ointment. "Now let me see to this so you can get some rest."

Thankfully, the medicament eased her pain as it soaked into her skin. Even so, it took a while to apply it to all the wounds. There was not a place left unmarked down her back and buttocks and thighs. Sitting on that horse must have been hell. Wearing garments must be hell. Hell, every moment must be hell. Finally, he finished and helped her put her shift back in place.

"Rest now," he said, pointing at the pallet. He gathered a few more blankets and watched as she knelt on the bedding and then lay down on her side, having a care not to lean on her back. "I want to sort through what we have and then take a look around the area." And beat someone to a bloody pulp. And curse the heavens. And call for a war against the damned MacLeod. His anger must have shown there on his face, for Isabel frowned.

"Alex?"

"All will be well, love," he said, going to her and kissing her gently. "I will see to my tasks and return quickly. If you have need, just call out my name. I will never be far."

He moved quietly around the small chamber, sorting through the food and extra clothing he had brought along. They had enough for several days before he would need to seek more. Alex listened until her breathing grew even and slow and then left the cottage. He strode away, wanting to hurt something, someone, for what had happened to his brave Isabel. For fear of being heard, he held his fury inside and, instead, thought about his wife.

A strange thing happened then. He realized he must not react in anger. He must be the one to protect her and get them away. Anger could not accomplish that, so he must put it aside and see her to safety. He must convince his father of the seriousness of his vow.

He must be the man she needed him to be.

CHAPTER 6

Ranald MacLeod paced in front of the table in his hall.

Around him, the keep stirred to life as it did every morn and he was there to greet it. Every morn. He liked the quiet and solitude of the mornings here in the hall. No one to blather at him. No one to bother him with questions or stupid words. And they knew not to approach him until he called for his food and ale.

He had slept well last night, finding a woman waiting in his bed had eased him into rest for the first time since he had ordered Evanna to watch over his disobedient daughter. This one, what was her name?, did not have to same skills at pleasure as his leman, but she had a plump, soft body, a hot mouth and a tight cunny, both of which he used well.

And truly, what more did a man need in his bed but someone warm and tight? Mayhap he could get Evanna to teach this one that trick she did with her tongue that pleased him so much. Mayhap he would have both of them in his bed now that his defiant daughter had been taught the first of the hard lessons he had planned.

Isabel would next find her betrothed was a man who believed, as he did, that women needed to ken the cost of disobeying or disrespecting their master. With the betrothal done, Ranald would give her over to Grigor MacKinnon's control. Then, he smiled thinking on it, her lessons in obedience would continue under a man of his own ilk and with an iron hand.

Now though, a buzzing of servants and guards interrupted his carnal thoughts and plans and he could ignore them no longer.

"What in the bloody hell is going on? Why are you disturbing me when you ken I have no wish to be disturbed in the morn?" he yelled.

Though it slowed their babbling, they did not go away. Ranald held out his hand for his cup of ale and walked to sit at the table. That was when he spied Evanna in the midst of the servants and guards waiting on his word.

"Evanna, what are you doing here?"

He motioned to her to approach and when she did not do his bidding quickly enough, he nodded to the guard. The guard spared no time or effort trying to be easy with her—he simply grabbed her by her arm and dragged her to Ranald.

"What is this about? Why are you not with my daughter?"

"My lord," she began, her voice trembling with true fear. It both intrigued and excited him. She knew how to beg and when to beg and how to plead her case. He missed her attentions in his bed. "Your daughter…"

"My daughter is … what?" From the fear on all their faces, Ranald knew he was not going to like the answer. He stood up, throwing his half-filled cup at her. She barely batted it in time but was covered with ale anyway. "Where is she?"

"My lord…"

He grabbed her hair and pulled her up so their faces were even, causing her to stand on the tips of her toes. Shaking her once and then twice, he repeated the question he should not have to repeat to any of those in his household.

"Where is Isabel?" he yelled so loudly that he swore the shutters on the windows in the walls shook.

"She … she … she …" The whore stuttered and stammered until he tossed her away.

"She is not in her chamber, my lord husband."

He whirled around to find his wife watching the whole scene. Only because she wore the same fearful expression as the others did he not strike her, too.

"They do not wish to be the one to tell you,"

Elizabeth said. "I went to tell her of her betrothed's expected arrival as you told me to do and found her gone."

"Gone where?" he asked of her before turning to the two people who should have been with his daughter at all times. "Where were you while my daughter was leaving her chamber?"

Evanna covered her head with her arms, waiting for him to strike. As he should. As he wanted to. As was his right. But now, he needed a clear head to decipher what was happening. So, instead, he stepped back and waited for her explanation.

"My lord, I was with her. As you ordered. Since you sent me to accompany her. The serving maid brought supper and I remember nothing after beginning the meal until your wi … Lady MacDonald came and released us."

"Released you?"

"They were asleep, tied up on the bedchamber's floor. Gagged as well." He narrowed his gaze at his wife.

'Twas clear she did not mind finding his leman so. Turning his attention to the guard, he asked, "When did you leave your post?"

"I did not, my lord," the guard began. "At least not that I remember."

This was very strange. Two people tied and gagged with no memory of how it happened. His daughter gone. Ranald watched as others arrived to break their fast but remained to see what would happen. Well, he had been embarrassed by his daughter here before and would not allow it again.

"Bring them," he ordered, pointing at his leman and the guard. "Wife, join us." He stopped and called out to the commander of his guards. "Close the gates. Seal the keep. No one comes or goes until I say so."

Elizabeth nodded without meeting his gaze as he expected. He had brought her to heel long ago and she would not dare disobey him now. Cowed. Obedient. At his feet. Like his best hunting bitch but less useful now that she could no longer bear him children and had never given him the son he wanted.

They gathered in the tower and he inspected his daughter's chamber alone first. Nothing was amiss here. No struggle had taken place. The bonds that had held his leman and the guard lay in a pile by the bed. Last night's tray sat on the table, scraps and bits still in the bowls.

Something was missing. Surely. He glanced around the room slowly knowing that something would be a clue to what had happened. Ranald lifted and smelled the bowls. He could detect nothing unusual in what was left over. He reached out and lifted the pitcher of wine. It was empty.

Not only was it empty, it had been rinsed out.

Checking, he discovered the cups in the same

condition.

Strange that. His daughter usually drank watered ale. The leman would drink wine, but never that much. And even a pitcher of wine would not have robbed the guard and the whore of their memories. Isabel had used something in the wine to make them sleep.

"Search her belongings."

And they found nothing out of the ordinary—no potions or bottles that could cause such a sleep.

It took hours but Ranald left the chamber with more knowledge about the possibilities than when he entered it. In his experience, the truth would out in the end, but the middle needed to be filled with just the right amount of force, threats and pain. With the correct balance, most any hidden knowledge could be outed.

The most surprising thing he had learned was from Evanna. Though she would suffer for keeping it from him as long as she had, the whore revealed that his daughter thought she was carrying.

Which meant a man had dared to ruin his daughter.

So, the tidiness of her disappearance now made more sense to him and he knew she must have had help to get away. Who would be bold enough to do something like this? Who would defile his daughter and then take her from under his watch?

With the betrothal to a MacKinnon, they would not

have done so and risk the dowry she would bring. That left only one other clan on the isle to consider— the MacDonalds. His family's oldest enemy and the clan whose leader carried the title Lord of the Isles. Had that old bastard sent his nephew's man in to ruin Ranald's heiress? To insult him personally? To stir up a war between them or to reclaim lands lost to them? They were the only ones foolish enough or, possibly, strong enough to take on the MacLeods.

He would quietly send trackers south toward the MacDonald keeps and lands on Skye even while searching his own. They would find Isabel and those behind this. No one, especially not a MacDonald, played The MacLeod for a fool.

CHAPTER 7

They had talked for hours, well into last night. Alex had taken care of her wounds again before they sought their bed and it helped the pain and tightness in her skin. Then, he had helped her to her side and lay next to her so carefully, it made her smile. Isabel could feel the caution he used so that his embrace did not hurt her more. He'd wrapped his arms around her so carefully and held her body close to his as they sought rest.

And they'd kissed. And touched. But they sought not a passion consummated but the extraordinary comfort in being alone with each other. With their fingers entwined, her body next to his, even their breaths mingled.

The words spoken had little to do with the danger around or trailing them and more to do with connecting once again where they had left off when they parted more than a month ago. Soft words.

Promising words. Silly love words.

Then they had slept. Even with the shutters closed on the small window of the cottage's wall, she could tell it was now nigh to midday. The fog had thickened yesterday as they rode, covering them but making their journey slower than Alex had hoped. She watched his movements as she sat on the small but comfortable pallet in the corner as he paced the small chamber.

His body was honed and muscled. Lean and tall, he walked with the grace of a predator, light on his feet and always … ready. Garbed or naked, he was a delight to watch.

"This kind of fog means a storm is coming," she said, finally gathering her wits from her shallow perusal of him. Having lived on the coast surrounded by the sea, Isabel knew the patterns and the signs. A storm could blow in off the sea at any time, but this thick blanketing mist that swirled in the wind foretold of one.

"Aye," he said, nodding at the sound of the wind. "We are far enough inland that the worst of it should not reach us." He turned to her and smiled. "And we have enough supplies to keep us fed for a few days here." Isabel stood and walked to him.

"So this was your plan? To hide here."

"Nay. This is only a respite. For you to gain your strength for the rest of our journey."

He leaned over and lifted her chin. A gentle kiss on her lips surprised her. After having to hide their affections, this felt good to her. To be within his reach and to be able to speak to him and to accept his caresses.

"The dark circles under your eyes tell me you are exhausted," he said softly, kissing her cheeks. "And the way you collapsed into sleep earlier, speaks of your need to rest."

Her stomach let out a grumble and she watched the smile burst forth on his face. His blue eyes flashed and the smile softened the strong, masculine angles of his face.

"And we should deal with your hunger." She laughed then, safer and happier than she had been in weeks. The hunger in her belly was a good sign. "There are some bannocks already made." He crouched down and search through one of the sacks. Finding what he looked for, he held out a smaller parcel to her. "Plain, but they will fill your belly."

"I fear we might starve if you depend on me to cook," she admitted. "'Tis a thing I have never learned to do." She unwrapped the cloth and found some flat oatcakes there. Taking one, she bit into the crisp wafer and chewed.

"You cannot cook?" he asked, mocking filled his tone. "The daughter of The MacLeod has never mastered that skill?" His wink belied his voice. "Well, any good Highlander knows how to make a bannock and a decent porridge."

"Even *The* MacDonald's *son*?" she asked back, laughing.

"Aye, even his beloved second son can do that task." He accepted the parcel when she handed it back and took a bannock from it. "I will teach you," he offered.

When her stomach made its emptiness known again, Alex tilted his head back and laughed. "Worry not, I will see your belly filled before we try it."

The oatcakes were gone within a few minutes, as was a small wedge of cheese he had packed away. He held out a skin of water to her and she quenched her thirst with it.

"Would you like to walk a bit before the rains come?" he asked, holding out his hand to her. "From what I've been told, you have been kept in your chamber for most of the last weeks." She took it and let him help her to her feet. "You might enjoy the brisk air."

"I would." That had been the best of part of their journey for her. In spite of its necessity, it had been the first hours she had spent outside a building since … since before …

"You will tell me if I walk too quickly or if you are tired?" he asked.

It felt so wonderful to have someone worrying

over her comfort that tears filled her eyes at his words. She could only nod in reply. He lifted the latch on the door and opened it for her. The winds blew and the fog swirled, but she did not care. Guiding her cloak around her shoulders and pulling the hood up, Isabel took his hand as they walked down the hill towards the stream and then along it for a short distance.

Although they had spoken of many things, reacquainting themselves to each other, Alex had not explained the rest of his plan. Or where they would go.

"Tell me, Isabel," he said before she could say anything. "What do you think your father will do? By now, he knows you are missing and not in the keep or village."

She shivered then, thinking on his wrath. If he had thought her disobedience was an insult, she could not fathom his reaction to her disappearance. A pang of guilt struck her then, forcing a gasp out to mingle with the mist around them.

"Are you ill?" Alex asked, turning to her, ready to aid her.

"Nay, not me." Isabel shook her head. "I just realized that I left Evanna and the guard to face my father's fury." The food in her stomach rebelled at the thought of what he could and would do to them for failing.

"Either of them would have done whatever they

needed to do to you, Isabel," he said softly, leaning in and touching his lips to her temple. "There was no other way to get you away safely."

"My father will seek retribution against anyone involved. Whether it is you or me and Evanna or anyone who helps me, it will be terrible."

"Then," he whispered, kissing her forehead before releasing her, "'tis a good thing you and I are not in his grasp."

He stepped away from her and she fought to control the fear that raced through her, making her tremble. If he had been lashed the way she had been, she knew he would be fearful, too. He entwined their fingers and held her arm near as they continued walking. Some of the tension in her dissipated as they meandered in the mist, following the water's edge along the burn. Mayhap when she knew the whole of it, she would feel less afraid?

"Alex, tell me of our plans." He nodded and guided her over a boggy place on the ground to part of the path that was drier.

"Brodie heads back to Knock Castle to tell my father about our marriage. In about a week's time, he will meet us on the other side of Skye, near Kilmalaug Bay, to take us home … or to the mainland to my cousin."

"Will Brodie be safe?" she asked. If his father were as ruthless and brutal as hers, no doubt Brodie would be endangered just delivering such news. She hoped Eoin MacDonald would not fault the messenger for the message.

"My father can be a right bastard when he wants to be," he admitted to her. "He is canny though and will listen and decide the matter on the facts of it."

Alex's tone and expression told her that he believed that. She had seen her father deliberate on clan matters and make decisions and knew that his approach was very different. She did not doubt that The MacDonald, nephew to the mighty Lord of the Isles, would find pleasure in tweaking her father's nose over this personal matter. The two powerful men, along with the head of the MacKinnons, ruled over the lands of Skye, playing one against the other in an endless game of power and control.

"If my father disowns me or disavows the marriage, I bring nothing to your clan, Alex." She stopped and faced him. "Why would your father support such a marriage for you?"

"I think there are many reasons he would. You are my wife, chosen and married, in fact. He will stand by me in this, as a matter of honor if nothing else."

"Alex, I should tell you—"

"Nay, Isabel." He touched a finger to her lips to stop her words. "If he does not, if he refuses to honor my vow to you, we will seek a place with my cousin. 'Tis known that the other branches of our clan have no love for my father."

Her fear about being pregnant and losing the bairn prevented her from forcing the news out. Nay, 'twas best to wait until she was certain, that there was no more bleeding or other signs of that condition, before sharing it with him. By then, they would be settled somewhere … together.

The winds picked up then and she could not help but shiver against it. It took little time for the warmer winds of summer to give way to autumn and then winter here. These storms could be vicious as they rolled off the sea and this one felt just that.

"Come," Alex said, taking her hand once more. "We should return to the cottage before the worst hits."

They were still some distance from the cottage when the mist turned to heavy rain and they began to run to take cover inside. Though out of breath when he closed the door behind them, Isabel felt alive for the first time in weeks.

She watched as he added some blocks of peat to the small hearth to warm against the growing chill. He stood and stretched, tossing his cloak over the pile of supplies and then hung hers on a peg by the door.

Something shifted within her then and she knew that she needed his touch now. Not the gentle, soothing caresses of last night. Nay, she needed to feel their passion course through her blood. She needed him to reclaim her body even as he held her heart.

"Alex?" she whispered, drawing his gaze to hers.

"Isabel?" Again, love and concern filled those eyes as he searched her face.

"Kiss me, Alex. Just kiss me."

His momentary hesitation tore her apart. Was he so put off by her condition and the way her back looked that he no longer desired her? Guilt followed that seed of doubt for he had not shown any reluctance before this.

Then he strode across the small space between them, stopping so close she could feel the heat pouring off his body. He leaned down as she tilted her face up to his.

"You want me to kiss you?" he asked in a voice deeper than usual. Before she could say a word, he stared into her eyes. "But ken this--'twill be more than one kiss, Isabel. More than kisses as well."

"I want to feel something other than pain and fear, Alex. I need to. So, aye," she said, sliding her arms up around his neck. "Kiss me."

CHAPTER 8

He had never heard more precious words. She wanted him. In spite of the terrible cost of loving him, she wanted him.

And God knew, he wanted her. His hands shook as he drew her closer and touched his lips to hers. Remembering where her wounds pained her the most, he avoided touching her there as he took possession of her mouth and thrust his tongue in to taste her deeply. Had she grown sweeter in their month apart?

When she sighed against his mouth, accepting his kiss and opening more to bring him in deeper, Alex fought for control. Whether or not she desired this, him, she was wounded and he needed to have a care for her. He moved his hands up to cup her head as he kissed her mouth and then slid down to taste the line of her jaw and the sensitive place below her ear. Her shiver and moan spoke of his success in arousing her.

His body hardened and his muscles tensed with

each sound and each taste. His cock rose, ready to fill her. His mouth watered as the thoughts of what he would like to do raced through his mind.

Everything, it whispered. *All of it. Leave no place on her untouched, untasted, or unclaimed.* Oh, he could very easily do that and spend the hours here exploring her so thoroughly that he could make her respond to even his voice. But …

This could not be that night. This needed to be one of pleasure and comfort for her. Alex drew back, loving the breathlessness of her when he did. Her lovely green eyes almost glowed as she watched him. Her lips already looked well-loved and he had only begun. Sliding his hands into her long blond hair, he loosened her braid and drew the locks around her.

"Let me," he said as she reached up and tugged on the laces of her gown.

He batted her hands away and smiled. Though it would be easier for him to lift both her gown and shift up and off, it would hurt her to move that way, so he unlaced the gown down the front until he could slide it off her shoulders. His hands may have shaken as he loosened the shift and pushed it down.

Following its path down her body, he caressed her breasts and belly and thighs as the cloth fell. She arched against his hand, her legs easing apart and asking for more. His mouth moved along the same path, her nipples tightened when he licked and then suckled them. And the sounds, the wondrous sounds of arousal and pleasure she made, spurred his own desire higher and higher.

Her belly rippled as he kissed there and he felt her hands tangle in his hair, grasping and pushing him on, when he reached the flaxen curls that guarded the center of her. Kneeling before her, he pressed his mouth there and he glided his fingers between her thighs and into the heated wetness.

She rocked her hips then, sliding away and then back against his hand. Her own hands became frantic in his hair and held his face against her. Alex needed to be inside her. As though hearing his thoughts, she gasped out.

"Take me, Alex. Come inside and finish this, I pray you!"

She had never been reticent or shy about their joinings or their mutual pleasure and he offered a prayer of thanks that she was not now. He leaned back on his heels and looked up at his beloved. Isabel looked like a goddess then, standing naked before him—her skin flushed with arousal, her nipples taut and tight and her eyes dark and dusky now.

He wasted no more time then. He tugged his shirt off and loosened his belt, dropping the length of plaid to the floor as he stood before her. Her gaze dropped to his hardened flesh and it pulsed in reaction. He did not bother with his boots. Alex took her hands in his and stepped back until the pallet was at his feet. Then, he climbed backwards onto it and eased her to her knees over him. She smiled when she understood what he was doing.

"Will this be an easier way?" he asked, even as she moved closer, bringing her heated flesh over his cock. Alex leaned over and suckled on one dark rose nipple and then the other, loving the way her body arched against his mouth.

"Aye, aye, aye," she whispered, with each slide of her body.

Her words became a chant that urged him on. Alex eased his hand between them and stroked the heated folds of her woman's flesh. Slow then faster. Gentle then harder. Along the outside and then into her flesh. Her expressive face told him when he was doing it right for her. Those green eyes drifted shut and her head tilted back as he pleasured her. Isabel's mouth opened as her breaths came in panting gasps, faster and faster until he knew he needed to be deep inside her.

He lifted her forward and slid his cock in, her hips canting so he could enter. Gasp followed gasp until her breathing became one long inhalation as she slid down his flesh, taking him all inside her body. His cock swelled then, her muscles surrounding his length and arousing it even more.

"Isabel," he whispered. "I am home."

She opened her eyes at his words and a single tear tracked down one cheek. He leaned forward carefully and kissed its path as it fell. Alex held her face in his hands, seated as deeply as he could be, and kissed her, pouring his love into her, as his seed would soon do. He lay back down then, drawing her with him until her golden hair fell around both of them like a curtain of the finest silk. Supporting her arms, he rocked his hips, sliding in and out of her tightness with each movement.

"Does it hurt you, love?" he asked, searching her face for any sign of pain.

"Nay, Alex." She smiled then, licking her lips and shaking her head. "It feels wondrous."

Their bodies soon found the rhythm they sought and everything within him grew tighter and hard. The center of her began to spasm around his erect flesh and she leaned her head back, moaning out a sound that filled his heart with joy and pleasure. He thrust faster and faster, deeper within her, over and over, until his seed poured out of him.

No words were spoken for several minutes. Isabel relaxed and lay over him, her breasts against his chest, their hips closed, and their flesh yet joined. She tucked her head under his chin and Alex reached up to gather her hair in his hand. Stroking her head, he whispered of his love.

Only a soft snore revealed that she slept there in

his arms, draped over him like the finest silk. His own body satisfied and his heart full, Alex dozed while she slept. A slight tensing was his first sign that she woke.

Isabel came to her senses, warm and relaxed and in less pain than she had felt in weeks. She should feel some embarrassment that she had fallen asleep on top of her husband, even while his male flesh remained within her. She should, but she did not.

"Are you well, Isabel?" he whispered. She heard his words and felt them rumble underneath her cheek where she lay against his chest. "Did I…"

She stopped his words with a kiss before he could ask her again.

"You did not hurt me, Alex." She kissed him again before trying to push herself off him. Truly, she should move since they were not … not … Or were they?

"Then, I pray you, stay," he urged. As he smiled at her, his cock began to harden within her.

Though they had loved and joined many times, this had not happened before. She tried to remain still as she felt his flesh fill her. Her inner muscles responded without her command, tightening around him in an echo of her recent release.

"Again?" she asked, enjoying the sensation of it.

"Only if you wish," he said, sliding himself out of her slowly. "You should rest."

He had taken such care not to hurt her while he saw

to her needs and his. Her heart felt revived after making love with him. Aches and pains had been replaced by such sweet pleasure and now he held back for fear of her comfort.

"Mayhap once more?" she teased.

He laughed then and dragged her face to his, kissing her deeply. She reached out to stroke his face and then slid her hands down to his hips. Every inch of him was strong. Every part muscled. And it was hers to enjoy. Isabel lifted her mouth from his to catch her breath and watched his face for a moment.

His mouth curved into a smile that would have tempted any woman. And it did and it had, as she had seen the first time she watched him in the village. He was an unabashed flirt, smiling and moving from woman to woman, plying his good looks much as a baker plied his bread. A tease here. Some playful words there. Within a short time, he had gathered quite a few admirers from the women who strolled through the market that morn.

She had been dressed not to be noticed there, enjoying a short respite from being the chieftain's daughter and walking amongst their village. Isabel had donned an unremarkable gown and worn a kerchief over her hair that day and still he smiled as he passed. Having seen him use his wiles on so many that morn, she laughed aloud when he smiled alluringly and greeted her.

At first, he had tried again and then a different ploy to make her fall over him as the others had. Then, when she just shook her head and laughed again at his antics, he changed. It was in that moment of change, when she glimpsed something within him that he hid from most, that she began to fall in love with him.

The next encounters and interludes together just confirmed it—for good or bad, familiar or stranger, she wanted him to be the one to whom she gave herself, heart, body and soul.

And now she had done that.

"I love you," she whispered as he moved within her. She pushed herself up as though to sit and he moaned then. Now she smiled. "Am I hurting you?"

He laughed aloud and shook his head, grabbing her by her hips. Now it was her turn to moan, for somehow, somehow, he managed to thrust deeper with just a move of his hips. But, he did it slowly and she could feel as each and every inch of him plunged into her and then withdrew almost to the tip. She was the one to cry out then and she clutched his hips by tightening her knees around him.

He wanted it slow. She wanted it fast.

In the end, they both won that battle for their loveplay continued for several hours, as the storm she had predicted would be bad was just that. But in their cottage, closed away from the world, it was just the two of them and, for a while, their troubles seemed to melt away.

When the morning arrived, clear and crisp and dry, Isabel felt better than she had in weeks. In the dark of the night, they had renewed their vows, one to the other and in the light of day she knew one thing— nothing or no one would ever part them again.

CHAPTER 9

They remained for one more day, enjoying the lull before the next coming storm that had little to do with the weather on Skye. Isabel remained at the cottage while Alex rode out to see if they were being followed. And to find additional food for the rest of their journey. Once rested, Isabel felt as though nothing could stop them.

"I have never been past Edinbane," she admitted as they set out for that small village.

"Never to Uig then?" he asked as they left the village and headed north and to the west now.

"Nay."

Isabel had traveled over the sea to one or two of the outer islands where her father held power, but never to this other side of Skye. These were heavily contested lands that switched back and forth, from clan to clan, every few generations depending on the whims of chieftains and kings. For now, that part belonged to the MacLeods.

"You have been here before?" She glanced at his face and saw guilt in his gaze. "What did you do?" He seemed surprised by her question, but then laughed.

"My brother asks me that question in the same way you just did—expecting me to confess my sins readily."

"Do you have sins to confess?" The words escaped before she could stop them. "I have no right to ask that, Alex."

"Do not look so distressed," he said, tugging his reins to slow his horse. Coming next to her, he shook his head. "I may have committed many youthful transgressions, but I assure you, nothing compares to my current crimes of debauching and then stealing a chieftain's daughter."

She could feel the heat rise in her cheeks at the memories of his debauchery with her.

"But, to answer your question, aye, I have been to Trotternish lands before. My brother and I went on a quest in response to a challenge by our cousins."

"How old were you?" she asked as they continued along the road. Alex was a wonderful storyteller and she could not wait to hear this tale.

"I had about twelve years and my brother three more when we crept through and around your father's lands to visit the places that used to belong to our family. Have you heard of Duntulm?"

A shiver raced along her skin at the mention of the ruined castle that faced the Minch. It had fallen out of use and into disrepair many years before because of several mysterious deaths and the stories told about ghosts that now haunted the place.

"I see you have," he said. "My cousins laid bets that we could not spend a day and a night there."

"And did you?" Curious because she had heard others who had tried and failed.

"Nay!" He laughed loudly then and shrugged. "Two brave lads, even my brother and me, could not stand up to the spirits that inhabit that place. The shrieks, the cries? Nay, we lasted until sunset before we pissed ourselves and got out of there."

Isabel laughed at his honesty over his failure. She could picture two boys trying to be brave and being scared witless, instead.

"Were your cousins there? Did they witness your … failure?"

"Oh nay, they wisely remained back in Sleat."

"And they won the wager? You told them the truth of it instead of embellishing what had happened?"

He frowned then, an attractive mix of horror and insult and humor, and shook his head at her, denying her accusation.

"I am a MacDonald and we stand by our word. We may have left out the pissing part, but we admitted our failure." Another laugh followed. "We made the same wager to them, but our fathers found out. We did not return to Duntulm or, alas, sit much for a long time after that."

They continued along the road and reached Uig late the day. As they had in Edinbane, they sought refuge in a secluded place off the road to keep away from prying eyes. For Isabel, it was a chance to become more familiar with her husband before they were forced to meet their fates. As the days passed and as Kilmalaug neared, she wondered if her father would catch up with them before they escaped.

For now, they were simply two travelers along the roads of Skye.

The weather that had gifted them with clear and chilly days changed as they reached the place where the road would turn north. A thick fog rolled into place around them and it was nigh to impossible to see but a few feet ahead of themselves. After a few hours of attempting to get through it, Alex brought them to a halt.

"We have but another hour or two of light anyway," he said. "I like it not, but we will camp here this night."

Instead of being secluded, they were near the road and could see no place to shelter in the mist. The sound of the sea was louder here, so they were close to it.

"I have no wish to walk over the edge of a cliff,"

she said, nodding in agreement.

Darkness overcame what daylight there was soon after they found a place and Alex laid out some blankets in a makeshift pallet for them. He built a fire for a bit of added warmth, but the dampness did not favor keeping it burning without constant care.

"Leave it," she said, holding out the thick, woolen length of tartan she had wrapped around her. "You will keep me warm enough."

It took only a second for him to accept her invitation and soon they sat, huddled together, eating what was almost the last of their bannocks. Alex had managed to heat the last bit of wine before the flames sputtered out and it warmed her as she swallowed some.

Isabel first noticed the woman when the sounds around them stopped. Complete and utter silence surrounded them and neither the sounds of the sea and birds nor the winds disturbed it.

She did not walk towards them so much as she seemed to glide. At first, Isabel thought her old and wizened, but, as she grew closer, her appearance grew much younger until she seemed no older than Isabel was herself.

"Do ye seek shelter for the night?" she asked in a soft crooning voice that echoed around them. "From the cold and coming storm?"

Isabel felt Alex tense as he saw and heard the

woman. He slid his hand onto his *sgian dubh* in an instant, a protective gesture that somehow Isabel knew was not needed. He stood and helped Isabel to her feet, wrapping the tartan around her shoulders first. Isabel noticed the woman's sad smile as she witnessed Alex seeing to her comfort.

"Aye, mistress," Alex said. "But we are strangers here and ken not where to find a place to rest."

The woman turned her head towards the sea and stared off in silence for a long moment. When she faced them once more, Isabel could see terrible loss and pain in her gaze.

"Would you share our meal, mistress? 'Tis not much to offer but we would share it with you if you are in need." Alex's brow furrowed but he did not naysay Isabel's offer. Instead, he reached over and poured some of the warmed wine into a battered cup they had brought and held it out to her.

"'Twill warm you on the chill night."

The woman did not speak then, but only shook her head, declining their meager hospitality. There was a restlessness to this woman, as though she fought some battle to stay here or to go elsewhere.

"Do you live nearby, mistress?" Isabel asked. "Have you lost your way?"

Isabel could not figure out what or how she knew, but this woman had lost everything. She doubted there was a cottage or farm she claimed as hers. She wanted to reach out and offer comfort to this … lost soul.

The woman turned sharply and stared in the direction to where they would go then. She gasped and became agitated.

"Follow this path towards the sea. Seek comfort there," she said. "Take yer things, yer horses and shelter amongst the ruins. Go now, I pray ye."

"Ruins?" Isabel asked.

"Is that not Duntulm?" Alex stared into the swirling mists but neither of them could see past the woman. Isabel turned in shock as she waited for the woman's reply.

"Aye," she said. "Duntulm."

For a moment, Isabel thought the woman's form shifted and she was harder to see. The strange, thick fog was playing its tricks on them. Then the woman turned her gaze on Isabel and she could not breathe.

Eyes like the rippling and strange color of the iridescent lights in the winter's sky to the north met Isabel's stare. Then, the woman seemed to disappear and reappear several times. All the while, Isabel could not move.

"Ye must go there now," the woman said.

The woman reached out to touch Isabel yet 'twas not a hand Isabel saw. A band of swirling mist encircled Isabel's wrist. She could feel it as though it were someone's hand, but no hand sat there. Then, a moment later, Isabel felt nothing.

"Isabel."

Alex's voice was a whisper though she heard the alarm in it. Turning around, she saw the woman once more standing now before Alex, reaching towards him. The same mist encircled his arm then and he stumbled, as it seemed to pull him from his place.

"Ye must protect the wee bairn," the woman said. Her voice raised to a wail now, one that blended into the returning sounds of the sea and approaching storm. "Protect the bairn there."

Isabel's hand dropped protectively over her belly.

Did this woman ken she carried? How could she? Then, what began as a raised hand, pointing in the direction of the sea, became a bright swirl of fog that drifted against the winds. Alex strode to Isabel's side as she tried to understand it all.

"What does she mean, Isabel? What bairn?" he asked.

"I was not certain, Alex, so I did not tell you. I carry your child." Joy filled her at the sudden revelation. But how had this woman known?

"Come, Isabel," he said. "Grab what you can and I will get the horses."

Not a moment later, the sound of approaching riders could be heard. The fog and the sea and the strange crying sounds made it difficult to tell how far away they were. No matter, they were riding fast and foolishly through the fog.

She picked up several sacks, their food and skin of wine and tossed the plaid over her shoulder. She followed closely on Alex's heels, not wanting to lose him in the mist.

"Lady?" the woman spoke from just behind her, scaring Isabel. She turned to face the woman and found no one there.

"Alex! Wait." He stopped and listened with her.

"Lady, seek refuge in the lower chamber. 'Tis drier than the rest." The words floated around them, coming from all directions and yet none she could find. A strange caress moved over her belly then. "The bairn will be just fine now."

The woman now addressed Alex. "Sir, keep yer wife and babe away from the cliffs and windows in the storm," the voice warned. "And do not leave the castle until dawn. No matter what ye hear. No matter what happens."

Something pushed them then. A not-so-gentle nudging by the winds to get them moving. This was so strange and Isabel should be terrified. Alex led the horses carefully along the path they could now see until they reached the ruins' perimeter wall. He tied the horses there, within the shelter of a half-fallen wall, and then led her down and into the ruins of the ancient keep.

CHAPTER 10

Alex remembered this part of the structure. Connor and he had made it this far on their quest before being scared witless by the noises that seemed to come from the very stones of the walls. Still shocked and surprised, and more than a bit confused by what had just happened, he wanted to see Isabel safe. Though he should question the strange occurrences and the appearance of that mysterious woman, something told him to do as she bade him do to save Isabel.

And their bairn!

Was that what troubled Isabel? He had seen her staring off into nothing and thought she was struggling with pain or the loss of her family and life. Had she been worried about a bairn? And how had she managed to carry it through the vicious whipping she had endured? He had so many questions, but first he must see to their safety for the night.

He found one inner chamber intact, part of the door

even hung from the hinges, so he helped Isabel inside. 'Twas only then that he noticed the candles flickering in the chamber. And the ones along the corridor they had followed went out as he closed, or rather lifted the door into place to block the winds.

"Did you see anything like that woman here when you and your brother snuck in years ago?" Isabel asked. Her head was tilted and her gaze questioning.

"That is not the first question that needs an answer, Isabel," he said, walking to her. The corners of her mouth curved up into an enticing smile and then she nodded.

"I thought I had lost it," she said softly. He watched her hand move as though to shield her belly in that unconscious movement of pregnant women. "I bled after the whipping but my normal courses never came."

"You never said," he whispered, lifting his hand to caress her cheek. "I …"

"There was nothing you could do," she explained. "Then, as I healed and the fever left me, I realized I'd missed three months." He counted backwards and smiled.

"Our wedding night."

"Aye, that night." A lovely blush filled her cheeks then.

"How did that woman ken?"

Part of him already knew the unbelievable answer

and part could not accept it. Had Isabel seen the same strange things he had? The way the woman faded from sight at times and seemed made only of fog and mist? The way the storm had seemed to wait on her? The way she had known that Isabel carried his child?

Before she could answer him, the winds picked up outside and a loud and mournful wailing began. His skin broke out in gooseflesh at the very sound of it. He reached over and pulled Isabel close to him when she shivered. If that sound made him ill at ease, the very-human screams that followed and melded with it were worse.

"What is happening?" Isabel whispered.

"She is protecting us, Isabel. As she promised."

"That woman was not … a woman, Alex." She had voiced what he had not.

"I think we have met the ghost of Duntulm," he said, understanding now who or what they had met out on the road.

If they had not known, the terrible shrieks and screams and the way the lightning crashed in time with the noises would have been a sign of otherworldly involvement. He held her until the sounds ended and the storm blew itself out to sea. After a time, they settled on some blankets on the floor, Alex holding her in his arms.

Would they see the ghost again? What had she done to those who were following them? As much as he wanted to ken, he did not wish to face her ghostly fury to find out.

The night passed and Alex could not sleep. The revelation of a coming child kept him awake even while Isabel slept next to him. His responsibilities had caught up with him and there was no way he could allow his father to turn his back on them now. He could not. He would not.

In the next hours, he thought on the arguments he would use to make his father understand, but it all came back to one—they had spoken marriage vows before God that he would not allow anyone to break apart. Regardless of her family or his, regardless of exile or remaining on Skye, they would do it together.

Just as dawn's light crept into the chamber from the corridor outside, a milky mist entered around the broken door and formed before his eyes. It was the ghostly woman.

"What is your name?" he asked in a quiet voice so he did not disturb Isabel's rest.

"Agneis MacDonald," the ghost replied, though whether she spoke aloud or he heard it in his own thoughts he knew not.

"Why are you here, Agneis?" Souls wandering had a task to carry out or were being punished for some wrongdoing. She began to sob then, a low keening sound that Isabel did not seem to hear.

"I was nursemaid to the laird's wee bairn," she

said. "During a storm, lightning struck the keep and I stumbled nearer to the window than was safe. The puir wee'un slipped through my hands." Tears streamed down her pale, almost-translucent face. "The laird cursed my soul to never find peace since he would not."

Pity struck him hard, making his own eyes burn and his throat tighten. Now that he knew about their coming child, he could almost imagine the horror of losing one in such a way. He could understand the laird's need to strike out. Still …

"How did you die, Agneis?"

The ghost began to twist her hands and rock side to side. His question had agitated her greatly.

"I beg your pardon for asking such a thing of you," Alex said. "No one should have to think on their own death."

Her response was unexpected and almost gleeful. The tears stopped and she smiled at him. She would have been a fine looking woman in her lifetime. Alex could almost see the color of her hair and her eyes.

"Ye heard them scream like bairns then?" she asked.

"Aye, we heard them." Alex nodded. "How many were there?"

"Nigh to a dozen." An eerie smile lit her features. "I separated them, each one from the others, and let them see their own deaths. They will not bother ye again."

His breath whooshed out at her words and Isabel startled. Agneis made a small gesture with her hand and whispered something that caused Isabel to sleep more deeply. Alex looked at Agneis, alarmed by this power.

"She needs her rest, ye ken?" Agneis came closer and touched Isabel's head. Gently. Carefully.

"Why did you help us?" he asked. "Can you never leave this place?"

"I couldna help my bairn. It happened so fast, there was not a thing I could do. But, I swore with my dying breath that I would help protect another's bairn if I could." Agneis smiled softly and shrugged. "I kenned she was carrying as soon as I saw her. Someone had to protect the babe."

"Well, you have my thanks, Agneis," he said. The calmness with which he sat speaking to a creature of legend amazed him. "I wish I could do something for you."

"Och, no matter. I am here until the Almighty says otherwise."

Then, before he could say another word, the sound of a baby floated into the chamber. One old enough to walk and laugh and play, from the sound of it. Agneis heard it, too, and she spun around looking for the source.

"That's my wee bairn!" she said. "That's my

Robbie!" More childish laughter echoed and Agneis looked towards the corridor. "Could he be here?"

Her form disappeared and a few seconds later, Alex heard peals of laughter from upstairs. He eased himself away from Isabel and followed the happy sounds until he reached the top storey of the keep. All that remained was part of the wall and the bottom of a window.

The window where she had dropped the babe in her charge.

Now, as the sun rose, Alex watched two misty figures dancing there—Agneis held on to a child tightly and spun in circles.

"Ah, my boy! I hiv missed ye so verra much!" she said and then she kissed the boy. The boy laughed, grabbing Agneis' hair and letting her have her way. Agneis clutched the babe to her once more and smiled at Alex.

"Hiv a care for yer son, Alexander MacDonald. Yer family comes for ye now." Agneis nodded to the north, towards Kilmalaug Bay.

They drifted up over the keep, becoming harder and harder to see in the sun's brightening light. Soon, they were nothing more than wisps of mist in the sky above. Alex stood staring, unable to believe what he had witnessed.

"Alex?" He turned and found Isabel there.

"Are you well?" he asked, sliding his arm around

her shoulders and bringing her close.

"I woke and thought I heard you speaking to someone up here."

"I was." He nodded above them at the now empty sky. "Agneis is gone now."

"Agneis? What happened?" He guided Isabel away from edge and back to the steps and below.

"Her name was Agneis MacDonald and a bairn in her care died. The father cursed her soul." Alex smiled at Isabel. "I think that by protecting our child, she broke the curse and her soul was released."

"Did she tell you that?"

"Aye, while you slept. It was the most wondrous thing, Isabel. We heard the sound of a child laughing and she went to him. They were together at last."

Then he realized the bit of news Agneis had given him in her parting words. He would keep that to himself and tell her later when they could savor it. Now, they needed to get to the bay and meet Brodie and the others.

"Come," he said, gathering up their belongings and holding out his hand to her. "Our journey is almost at an end."

CHAPTER 11

'Twas not Brodie who greeted them on the shore at Kilmalaug Bay after all. A huge man with muscled arms and a severe expression watched their approach and he was none too happy from the look of him.

Isabel shivered then at the sight before her.

Alex had spoken of one boat, a small birlinn mayhap, coming to help them escape. Not one but four larger boats sat in the bay there. All carried the banners of the MacDonalds. So, that meant that this man could only be…

"Isabel, may I make you known to my father, Eoin MacDonald of Sleat?" Alex's voice was calm as he spoke the words, but she could feel the tension in his hand that held hers.

His father closed the space between them in two long strides. From his appearance alone, she should be terrified of him. He was carrying every weapon a warrior could carry and seemed every bit ready to use them all. And yet, the funniest thought came to her in that moment. She smiled as she bowed her head to him.

"Father, may I present to you, Lady Isabel MacLeod, my wife?" A moment of silence was followed by sheer mayhem.

"Wife?" his father yelled.

"Wife!" another man who looked remarkably like Alex called out. He pushed others out of his way to approach them. Before Alex could stop him, the man took her hand and pulled her into his arms, squeezing the very breath from her. "You married her? You married her!" he yelled.

"Connor, let go of my wife," Alex ordered in a growl.

Connor. Oh, this was his older brother, Connor! Before he released her completely, he leaned in and kissed her on her cheek.

"If I had known you were this bonny, I would have agreed to marry you myself, lass."

Alex finally managed to pry her loose from his brother and she was left facing his father. Her husband entwined their fingers and began to speak.

"Father, we married three months past."

"And I am only finding out about it now?" His father crossed his massive arms over his chest and narrowed his gaze at both of them. "And 'tis not my son who tells me of his marriage to our enemy's daughter. Nay, 'tis Brodie.''

Isabel could not help but smile as this bear of a man growled at them. Any fool could see his love for his son there in his gaze. But men were not always able to see it, were they? Loosening her hand from Alex's, she stepped up to The MacDonald and placed her hand on his forearm.

"Aye, my lord. Your son married your enemy's daughter. And your enemy's daughter now carries your first grandchild in her womb."

Alex's father crumbled into laughter then, leaning over with his hands on his knees to support himself. Everyone else looked on in shock, not expecting this to happen, she could tell. After several minutes, the chieftain stood and grew serious once more. Alex stepped to her side and smiled proudly at her.

"I guess we'll have to keep you then."

As the others cheered, he motioned for Alex to come closer and whispered some fierce words to only him before he released her husband back to her. Then, with a wave, he summoned her to him. Alex tensed as though worried over what his father would do, but she did not worry. She walked to him, stopping only when she could go no further and then looked up and up and up to meet his gaze.

"Why did you smile when you saw me?" he asked.

"You are bigger than my father and his man, Gair. I knew you were the perfect one to be at my back if my father challenges my marriage to your son." She had surprised him and she knew it at once.

"How do you ken I will back this marriage?" he asked gruffly. "'Twill be more trouble than you ken."

"Because," she began, leaning in closer. "You love your son and will stand at his side when he needs you there." He shook his head as if denying it. "Come now, any fool with eyes can see it."

One moment she was watching him and the next she was being hugged to within an inch of her life. Alex grabbed his father's arms to try to free her, but even the pain could not make her give up this embrace. It felt so wonderful to have the support of this man, when she had never gotten it from her own father.

As big as he was, The MacDonald could be gentle, too, for when she gasped, he loosened his hold on her and then released her to Alex.

"Come. We saw more MacLeod warriors gathering a few miles back and one of their ships behind us." Eoin called out orders and within a shorter time than she thought possible, they were out to sea.

As they passed the cliffs where Duntulm sat, Alex kissed her. Staring up at the crumbling ruins there, she thought about the poor woman who had suffered so many years and was now free. In a small way, that could describe her own life. Isabel smiled then as the years ahead stretched out before them, much as the

miles of sea that surrounded Skye did.
Endlessly she hoped.

*Alex MacKendimen and Maggie Hobbs are both
attending a Highland clan gathering when they
accidentally meet near some ruins. Or is it
accidental after all?*

He took a step back from her and held out his hand in
a more recognizable gesture. She hesitated for a
moment and then shook it—American-style.

"I am Scottish but, as you can tell, I'm not from
here. I'm Alex MacKendimen, from the States."

"That answers my question of the day."

"What question?"

"What the real heir of the clan looks like. It's the
topic of the gathering."

He blushed. She didn't remember seeing a man
blush before, but it looked so darn attractive, she
hoped to see it again. The blush made his blue eyes
look a shade lighter than they were. Ruggedly
handsome features stood out on his tanned face. He
wore his hair, a shade of dark auburn with red
highlights that flashed in the strong sunlight, in a
conservative cut above his ears and short all around.
And the blush spread to the tips of his ears.

"I'm sorry," she said, "I didn't mean to embarrass
you."

"I really don't like being the center of conversation. But it's not your fault at all."

"Then whose is it?"

"Well, mine, I guess. I brought my aunt here for this reunion without knowing all the details."

"Details such as you're the lost heir of the clan?"

"No, not lost. They knew where I was all along."

She let herself join his laughter at his words, and Maggie realized she hadn't introduced herself.

"I'm Maggie Hobbs," she smiled as she said it, "also from the States."

"Nice to meet you, Maggie. From where in the States?"

"New Jersey."

"New Jersey? Really?"

"Yes, the good old Garden State."

"I don't believe it! Me too!"

"Really?" she asked, "Where?"

"I live in Haddonfield."

Maggie sat back down on the wall. "I live in Winslow. Can you believe it? We're almost neighbors and have to travel more than a thousand miles to meet." She shook her head at the irony of coming all the way to Scotland and meeting someone who lived close by.

"How did you turn up here?" Alex asked.

"I'm a teacher, and this is the first summer I'm not going to school. So, I came here for the history. And," she added in a low, conspiring tone, "I've wanted to visit here ever since I read my first Scottish romance novel. And you?"

"As I mentioned, I brought my aunt Jean back to attend the gathering. You know, she played on my sympathies to come with her, but I think she had this 'rightful heir' thing planned all along."

"Are you?" Maggie raised her eyebrows in question.

"The rightful heir?" At her nod, he continued, "Apparently. My father was the eldest son and would have inherited. But he refused his inheritance and moved to the States in search of the woman of his dreams."

"That sounds romantic. Did he find her?"

"Yes, he did. He married my mother a year after arriving. Anyway, I guess if he had stayed, I would be the heir of the clan. But...."

"Does the real, I mean, the proclaimed heir know that you're not going to challenge him?"

"I think Uncle Calum realizes I'm no threat to him. I am here to enjoy the gathering and meet the clan. But I am definitely not enjoying the dress." Had he noticed her gaping at his legs again? How embarrassing!

"Dress?" she asked, forcing her eyes back up to his face. "Don't you call it a plaid?"

"They can call it anything they want to, but I call

it too short and too damned drafty," He twisted the kilt at his waist and resettled his belt. He turned away from her and adjusted the long scabbard that hung from his belt and contained a sword. After another moment, he shifted again and pulled the sword from its cover. Alex placed it point down along his leg, resting it on his boot and holding onto its jewel-encrusted hilt. Then he sat on the wall next to her. "So, how long are you going to be here in Scotland?"

Maggie pushed her hair over her shoulders and sighed. "I'm nearly done. I have three more days in the Trossachs and Glasgow, four days in England, and then home. How about you?"

"We leave here at the end of the week and are spending a few days in Inverness. After that Edinburgh, and then home. By the way, do you have plans for dinner?" He extended the invitation without a moment's hesitation.

"Well, actually I do. My tour bus will pick me up, and I'll have dinner with the group." Not wanting to be rude and realizing that they would both be going back to the same area in New Jersey, she added, "Maybe we could get together when we're back home?"

"That sounds great. I just wish we had more time here." Sincere regret filled his voice. She heard it, felt it, and found herself hoping for the first time in their conversation that they would see each other again.

"Time?" A scratchy voice interrupted their conversation. Maggie never saw or heard Mairi's approach. Now, she stood directly in front of them, so close that they couldn't get up from the wall. Maggie felt the vibrations under and around her grow stronger. A buzzing sound, like a swarm of bees attacking a hive's enemy, surrounded them.

"Mairi, you startled me." Looking at Alex, she said, "Do you feel that?" She placed his hand under hers on the stones between their bodies. Even the stone wall beneath them carried the vibrations now.

"Feel what?" He frowned, obviously not feeling or hearing what she could.

"That pulsing and heat coming from the stones."

"I don't feel anything, Maggie." Alex looked back at Mairi. "Who are you?"

Before the old woman answered him, she placed one hand on both of them, on their shoulders.

"Time? Ye can have all the time ye need, lad. Remember, time will prove if a love be true."

Then, with a force completely at odds with the frailty of her figure, Mairi pushed them backward, through the arch.

I'm blind!

Blinking against the complete darkness and

fighting against the terror overwhelming her, Maggie's chest tightened. Unable to breathe, she reached up to rub her eyes, but her hands refused her mind's command to move.

Oh, God, blind and paralyzed. But how? A few... moments? minutes? hours? ago, she was sitting on that wall, talking to Alex. And now? Had she fallen and hit her head and done this to herself?

Just before utter and uncontrollable panic took over, she heard a voice: Mairi, the old fortune-teller from the festival. She struggled to call out to the woman, but her voice also failed her. She must have really banged her head hard because her hearing wasn't working well, either. Mairi's words weren't clear at all. She seemed to be mumbling about time. Time would prove... Time would prove what? A blinding flash of light roared through her darkness, and she could move once again.

"If love be true." Alex repeated aloud the words he just heard in that all-encompassing darkness. Finally able to move, he shielded his eyes against the brightness. Squinting, he raised his head and saw that he and Maggie were lying in a field. Scrambling to his feet, he reached down to help her stand.

"Are ye weel?"

"What did you say?" she asked. Her voice trembled as she accepted his help to stand.

"I said, 'Are ye weel?'"

He watched as her face scrunched up in an expression of complete confusion. Well, he wasn't feeling quite clear about this, either.

"Why are you talking like that?" she asked.

"Speaking how? I do not know yer meaning."

Her mouth hung open now, gaping in... surprise? Shock? What was her problem now? First, she seemed offended by his greeting when they first met and now... what?

"What is the problem?" he asked as he straightened, yet again, the damned plaid at his waist.

"Was it just an act? A line to pick up women?"

"A line? What are ye blabbering about?" He scratched his head. Obviously, their fall backward must have shaken them both. Maggie was making no sense at all.

"The one about being the missing heir of the clan? You are obviously Scottish, from here not America. I mean, you have such a strong brogue that I can hardly understand you!" She took a few steps away from him and crossed her arms over her chest, chin out in challenge.

"Are ye daft, woman? I told you, I am from New Jersey, just as ye are." He crossed his arms in a matching gesture.

"Look, no one I know in any part of New Jersey sounds like you do. If this is a game—try out an American accent and meet women—well, you can play by yourself." She grabbed her backpack off the ground, flung it over her left shoulder, and turned away from him.

That's when he noticed.

Everything was gone. The ruins, the tents from the festival, and all of the people. The only sounds in the air were the singing of some birds and rustling of the wind through the branches of the nearby trees. He spun around, looking up, down, through the trees, and off in the distance where the meadow seemed to end. Nothing. They were alone.

Maggie apparently noticed it at the same time because, as she turned back to him, all of the color drained from her face and she swayed slightly. Alex grabbed for her and helped her to sit down in the grass; then he joined her on the ground.

"I don't think I understand what's going on here, Alex."

"Well, I am not sure I know anything more than ye do, but let's try to figure out what's going on."

Maggie reached into her backpack and pulled out a small bottle of water. After taking a swallow of it, she offered it to him. "Are you really from here? Is your accent real?" she whispered as he took the bottle from her grasp.

"Please believe me, Maggie. If ye are saying that I hae a brogue, I do not understaun. I canna hear it. I am hearing my words in the English I hae always spoken."

"Alex, you now have an accent as thick as the seer woman at the festival. You really can't hear it?"

"Nay, Maggie. 'Tis clearly English to me," he pointed to his ear and head with his free hand, "in here. I swear to ye—'tis no line to pick up women. What seer woman do ye mean?"

"Mairi, from the festival. She said she has the sight."

"The old woman who was wi' us in the ruins?"

Maggie just shook her head and looked around at the empty field. "Where is she? Where is... everything?"

After he took a swig from the bottle and handed it back to her, tapping her on the shoulder with the bottle to gain her attention, he said, "We should probably move closer to the woods. We're out in the open here, and I do not hae any idea of what's going on. Let's get under some cover and then we can talk. Can ye walk over to those trees?"

At her nod, he helped Maggie back to her feet. His legs still felt wobbly, and his head was still spinning slightly. After standing for a few moments, he guided her to the edge of the field where the woods began. They used some large boulders as seats as they both surveyed the area.

"So, what's the last thing you remember?" she asked. The color was finally returning to her cheeks and she didn't look ready to faint anymore. Thank God. He was a wimp when it came to crying or fainting women.

"'Tis as I said before, I remember talking to that old woman while we were sitting on the wall. She was rambling on about something." He rubbed his forehead with the back of his hand and tried to clear his memory. "Time. She was saying something about the power of time. Does that make any sense to ye?"

"I remember sitting and talking to you. And I remember Mairi, too. Did she put her hand on your shoulder? I can kind of see her resting her hand on my shoulder... and pushing me backward? This doesn't make any sense at all." Maggie shook her head in confusion.

"She did push me backward!" Alex jumped up and started to pace. He always felt better if he could pace. "I remember losing my balance and grabbing for the sword to steady myself. The sword... Hae ye seen it?" With a hand on his forehead to shield his eyes, he scanned the field where they had been, looking for the laird's sword. The sunlight would reflect off the polished metal, making it easy to spot. "I do not see it."

Alex ran out onto the field and looked for the

claymore. "I flung it back o'er my head as I fell," he called out to Maggie as he walked quickly back to her. "I can remember thinking that I hoped no one was close by as I released my grip on it." He touched the empty scabbard on his belt.

"Okay," Maggie started, "we were sitting on the wall, Mairi pushed us backward, and we fell, landing where?"

"I do not hae any idea where. What do ye remember about the fall? Did ye hear or feel anything?" Alex probed, trying to come up with some plausible explanation of what had happened.

"I thought that I was blind—the darkness was that complete. I tried to move, and I couldn't. Breathing was even difficult, but that might have been because I was terrified." She shivered and blushed a little at her admission. "I tried to scream, but nothing came out. I heard Mairi, but her words weren't clear. Something like 'Time will prove.' How does that compare with your experience?"

"Ye hae pretty much described what I went through, too," Alex agreed. "And I heard, 'If love be true.' Now what can 'Time will prove if love be true' mean? 'Tis nonsense to me, how about ye?"

"It sounds like a proverb or old saying. Well, any suggestions about what we do now?" Maggie asked, still eyeing him suspiciously. He wished he could hear the accent she was hearing. Maybe then he could understand her misgivings.

"I guess, if ye are feeling up to it, we could try finding someone. Head in a direction and look for signs of civilization?"

"Sounds fine to me," Maggie said. "Maybe we can find someone who can explain what's going on and how we got to wherever this is."

Alex grabbed her hand and then paused to look at the sun. "'Tis the east. Let's head in that direction for a bit and see where it leads us."

Maggie took advantage of Alex's leading to try to collect her very scrambled thoughts. She knew that Mairi had said some strange things to her both during her "reading" and before they fell off the wall. She smiled to herself and hoped Alex didn't see it. This strange situation was no laughing matter, but falling off the wall just struck her in a funny way. What had happened to them? And, more importantly, what about him? Was he telling the truth about being from America? The accent sounded as authentic as any she'd head on her tour. None of this made sense.

Well, until they met up with people, she'd have no way of even guessing where they were and how they got there. But, at least, she wasn't alone. Although they had just met and she'd not liked some of his mannerisms, she felt very comfortable with Alex. Even holding his hand while they walked felt somehow familiar and reassuring. She realized that they were slowing, and she looked around.

"Why are we stopping? We couldn't have walked more than a half mile."

"Maggie, sshhhh. Do not ye hear it?" Alex whispered.

At first, the only sound she could hear was their breathing. That's when she noticed that the birds had stopped singing around them. She tilted her head back slightly and listened intently. Rumbles of thunder came from off in the distance, growing louder and closer.

"Thunder? A storm is coming this way?"

"No, Maggie, 'tis no' a storm. It sounds like a stampeding herd."

Maggie swallowed convulsively, her throat beginning to tighten as the fear built in her blood. "A stampede? But where is it coming from?"

Vibrations swelled and pulsed in the ground under her feet and her heart pounded to the same beat. She and Alex both turned to try to get a bearing on the direction of the sound when a flock of birds scattered into the air, frightened from the trees in the distance, off to their left.

The tension and terror and thunder in the air made it impossible for her to make her feet move. She looked over at Alex and watched as he tried to draw his missing sword against whatever was coming at them. The sounds grew louder and more terrifying until she fought to release the screams trapped inside of her. And then she could see, rampaging toward them, unbelievable images straight out of Scotland's past. The far past!

Meet Terri Brisbin

RWA RITA®-nominated, award-winning and *USA Today* best-selling author **Terri Brisbin** is a mom, a wife, grandmom(!) and a dental hygienist. Terri has sold more than 2.5 million copies of her historical and paranormal romance novels and novellas in more than 25 countries and 20 languages. Her current and upcoming historical and paranormal/fantasy romances will be published by Harlequin Historicals, St. Martin's Press/Swerve, PenguinRandomHouse, and independently, too.

Connect with Terri:
Facebook: TerriBrisbin
Facebook Author Page: TerriBrisbinAuthor
Twitter: @Terri_Brisbin

TerriBrisbin.com

Other Books by
by Terri Brisbin

THE MacKENDIMEN STORIES:
A Love Through Time
Once Forbidden
"A Highlander's Hope" in CHRISTMAS IN KILTS
A Matter of Time

THE DUMONT STORIES:
The Dumont Bride
The Norman's Bride
The Countess Bride ****
"Love at First Step", THE CHRISTMAS VISIT
The King's Mistress ****
"The Claiming of Lady Joanna", THE BETROTHAL

THE MacLERIE STORIES:
Taming the Highlander
Surrender to the Highlander
Possessed by the Highlander ♥
"Taming The Highlander Rogue" ebook
The Highlander's Stolen Touch
At The Highlander's Mercy
"The Forbidden Highlander" in HIGHLANDERS
The Highlander's Dangerous Temptation ♦
Yield to The Highlander

Related stories (same clan 500 years later)
The Earl's Secret
"Blame It On The Mistletoe" in ONE CANDLELIT
CHRISTMAS****

THE KNIGHTS of BRITTANY STORIES:
"A Night for Her Pleasure" ebook &
in PLEASURABLY UNDONE
The Conqueror's Lady
The Mercenary's Bride
His Enemy's Daughter

THE STORM STORIES:
A Storm of Passion
"A Storm of Love" ebook & *in* UNDONE
A Storm of Pleasure
Mistress of the Storm ∞

STAND-ALONE STORIES:
The Queen's Man
The Duchess's Next Husband
The Maid of Lorne
"Kidnapping the Laird" ebook & in MAMMOTH
BOOK OF SCOTTISH ROMANCES
"What The Duchess Wants" ebook & in
ROYAL WEDDINGS THROUGH THE AGES
"Upon A Misty Skye" in ebook, print & in ONCE UPON A
HAUNTED CASTLE ♦
"Across A Windswept Isle" in ebook & in FORBIDDEN
HIGHLANDS
A Traitor's Heart in BRANDYWINE BRIDES

NOVELS OF THE STONE CIRCLES STORIES:
Rising Fire ♥
Raging Sea
Blazing Earth

A HIGHLAND FEUDING STORIES:
Stolen by the Highlander
The Highlander's Runaway Bride
Kidnapped by the Highland Rogue
Claiming His Highland Bride
A Healer for the Highlander

***** RWA RITA® Finalist!!* ♥ *NJRW Golden Leaf Winner!!*
♦ *USA TODAY Bestseller!!* ∞*RomReviews Best of 2011*